# LAWMAN ON THE RUN

Slocum, Chaney and the rest walked back to the sheriff's office.

"The safe's standing open," Chaney said.

"It looks like he cleaned it out in a hurry," said Pearlie.

"Likely they headed out of town in that direction," said Slocum, pointing. "I don't think they'd ride toward where they knew we was at."

"We going after them?" asked Flank Steak.

Chaney looked toward Pearlie and then Slocum.

"Not all of us," Slocum said.

"I'll go," said Chaney, "and—"

"No," said Slocum. "You got a ranch to run, and now you won't have no one interfering with you. I'll go."

"At least take a couple of boys with you," Pearlie said.

"When I can't handle two like that by my own self," Slocum said, "I'll hang up my guns."

# JAKE LOGAN

## SLOCUM
## AND THE CROOKED SHERIFF

J

JOVE BOOKS, NEW YORK

**THE BERKLEY PUBLISHING GROUP**
**Published by the Penguin Group**
**Penguin Group (USA) Inc.**
**375 Hudson Street, New York, New York 10014, USA**
Penguin Group (Canada), 10 Alcorn Avenue, Toronto, Ontario M4V 3B2, Canada
(a division of Pearson Penguin Canada Inc.)
Penguin Books Ltd. 80 Strand, London WC2R 0RL, England
Penguin Group Ireland, 25 St. Stephen's Green, Dublin 2, Ireland (a division of Penguin Books Ltd.)
Penguin Group (Australia), 250 Camberwell Road, Camberwell, Victoria 3124, Australia
(a division of Pearson Australia Group Pty. Ltd.)
Penguin Books India Pvt. Ltd., 11 Community Centre, Panchsheel Park, New Delhi—110 017, India
Penguin Group (NZ), Cnr. Airborne and Rosedale Roads, Albany, Auckland 1310, New Zealand
(a division of Pearson New Zealand Ltd.)
Penguin Books (South Africa) (Pty.) Ltd., 24 Sturdee Avenue, Rosebank, Johannesburg 2196, South
Africa

Penguin Books Ltd., Registered Offices: 80 Strand, London WC2R 0RL, England

This is a work of fiction. Names, characters, places, and incidents either are the product of the author's
imagination or are used fictitiously, and any resemblance to actual persons, living or dead, business
establishments, events, or locales is entirely coincidental.

SOLCUM AND THE CROOKED SHERIFF

A Jove Book / published by arrangement with the author

PRINTING HISTORY
Jove edition / November 2004

Copyright © 2004 by Penguin Group (USA) Inc.

ISBN: 0-515-13852-5

JOVE®
Jove Books are published by The Berkley Publishing Group,
a division of Penguin Group (USA) Inc.
375 Hudson Street, New York, New York 10014.
JOVE is a registered trademark of Penguin Group (USA) Inc.
The "J" design is a trademark belonging to Penguin Group (USA) Inc.

PRINTED IN THE UNITED STATES OF AMERICA

10  9  8  7  6  5  4  3  2  1

# 1

Slocum had been riding for some days and had not had a good meal, a drink of good whiskey or a good cigar for even longer than that. He had used up all of his cash from his last job in his wanderings, so now he was looking for work. Any kind of work. He was moving along a road that would lead eventually to a small town called Hangout. He thought that he might find something there, but then he came across a large arched sign over an open gateway. It read, "Snug T Ranch." He stopped and studied the sign for a moment, then turned his horse under it and onto the lane that ran on into the Snug T.

The narrow lane curved around a grove of trees and wound its way up to the front of a big ranch house with a porch that stretched all the way across the front. The porch was covered by an upstairs balcony. As he approached the house, Slocum could see that the porch and the balcony above it were dotted with several chairs and tables. The place was certainly designed for someone's comfort. Back behind the house and off to its right was a long bunkhouse, and near the bunkhouse was what appeared to be a cook shack. Not too far away from the bunkhouse was the corral. Slocum could see several fine-looking horses in the corral, and at one end was a large barn.

The whole look of the place was clean and neat. It was a

prosperous ranch. He could tell even at a glance. As he rode closer, he saw a young woman step out onto the balcony. She seemed to have gotten a look at him and disappeared back into the house. As Slocum came up close to the big porch, a man dressed in a fine suit stepped out. He had a pipe in his mouth and was sending up smoke signals. His hairline was a little receding, and he wore a small mustache. He stood waiting casually, his hands in his pockets. Slocum hauled up close to the porch and stopped his big Appaloosa.

"Hello, stranger," said the natty man on the porch. "You're welcome here. I'm Reginald Tyson. This is my ranch."

Slocum touched his hat brim. "Howdy, Mr. Tyson. My name's Slocum."

"Been riding long, Mr. Slocum?" Tyson asked.

"Long enough."

"Climb down. Come up on the porch and sit. I'll have you a cup of coffee in a minute. You do drink coffee?"

"I do when it's available to me."

"Ah, very good, Mr. Slocum," said Tyson. He stepped over to the door, opened it and called into the house. "Pearlie, could you bring some coffee out here? Two cups, please."

Slocum took a chair, and Tyson turned back toward him. He walked over and sat facing Slocum.

"If you don't mind, Mr. Tyson," Slocum said, "I ain't never been called 'mister.' Folks just call me Slocum."

"Very well, Slocum. I've been out west long enough to know that I should never ask where a man has been, but may I ask, are you a cowhand? You have that look about you."

"I've done some cowpunching," said Slocum.

"And I bet you're good at it."

"I can handle my end all right."

The door opened and the young woman Slocum had seen briefly on the balcony came out onto the porch with a tray. On the tray were a pot, two cups and small items that Slocum took for a creamer and a sugar container. There were also a couple of spoons. She put the tray down on a table there between the two chairs.

"Thank you, my dear," Tyson said. "Mr.—excuse me—Slocum, this is my niece, Pearl Tyson. Pearlie, dear, meet, uh, Slocum."

"Just Slocum?" said Pearlie.

"Just Slocum, ma'am," Slocum said, standing and taking off his hat. "I'm pleased to meet you."

Pearlie made a slight curtsy. "Likewise, I'm sure, Slocum," she said. "Anything else, Uncle?"

"No, dear. Thank you."

"Then if you'll excuse me," Pearlie said, and not bothering to finish her sentence, she turned and walked back into the house. Tyson gestured toward the tray.

"Please, Slocum," he said. "Help yourself."

Slocum poured himself a cup of coffee and picked it up for a tentative sip. It was hot, but it tasted just fine.

"No cream or sugar?" said Tyson.

"No, sir," said Slocum. "Thanks."

Tyson poured himself a cup and sugared and creamed it. He took his pipe out of his mouth and put it on the table. "Will you stay for lunch with us, Slocum?" Tyson asked.

"Thank you," Slocum said. "To tell you the truth, I was kind of hoping you'd ask. Like I said before, I've been on the trail for a few days. Last meal I had was a scrawny jackrabbit and some water."

"Oh dear," said Tyson. "We'll have to fix that. May I ask, are you by chance looking for work?"

"I could use a job," Slocum said.

"It happens that I'm a bit shorthanded just now. But I should be honest with you. There's bad blood between me and another rancher. So far nothing has come of it, but I've had some boys quit because they were afraid that something might happen. It's a bit of a tense situation."

"What seems to be the problem?" Slocum asked.

"Well, LeDoux, that's the other rancher, has had Army beef contracts for some years, and when I moved into these parts a couple of years ago, I beat him out on the contracts. He doesn't like that. He's also had the only store in Hangout, and he's been charging outlandish prices. I decided that had gone on long enough, so I built my own store. Undercut his prices. I must say, he's not happy with what I've been doing."

"I see."

"Does that frighten you off?"

"I don't scare easy, Mr. Tyson," Slocum said. "I'll take the job."

"Good. The boys will be in for lunch soon. You'll have lunch here in the house with me and Pearlie today. After we've eaten, I'll take you over and introduce you around. My foreman's name is Al Chaney. He's a good man."

"I'll be glad to meet him," Slocum said.

Off in the distance, some of the cowboys were riding in toward the bunkhouse. Slocum figured it was about lunchtime. It couldn't come too soon for him. He finished off his coffee and put the cup down on the tray. Tyson stood up. "Would you like to wash up before we eat?" he asked.

"Yeah. I would."

"Come along then, and I'll show you where you can do that."

Tyson led the way into the house. In a matter of a few minutes, Slocum, somewhat freshened up, was seated at a sumptuous table with Tyson and the lovely young Pearlie. He tried to concentrate on the food on the table and on his plate, and it was a good meal, but it was prepared by the delicate hands of the sweet thing sitting across from him. He couldn't keep his eyes off her. She was a blonde with blue eyes, but she seemed bright enough in spite of that seeming drawback. She had a fetching smile, sweet but showing a little something, a hint of the cynic maybe. Her ample bosoms heaved beneath a low-cut blouse with each breath she took. Enough of them showed to make Slocum want to see more. When she got up to go back to the kitchen for something or other, her monumental round ass rolled inside her tight jeans. Slocum bit his tongue and concentrated, or tried to, on his meal.

"So you're going to work for us?" she said as she returned to the table.

"Yes, ma'am," he said.

"Please," she said as she sat back down. "If you don't want me calling you Mr. Slocum, you'll have to call me Pearlie."

"All right, Pearlie," he said.

He lifted his coffee cup for a sip. It also gave him the opportunity to raise his eyes over the cup and feast them with a look at Pearlie. She was looking at him and caught his gaze. She smiled. Slocum saw that as a sign of encouragement. He knew that he would be sleeping in the bunkhouse and taking future meals with the cowhands at the cook shack, but that simply presented him with a challenge. He recalled that sumptuous ass rolling around in the tight jeans, and he really wanted to mount her. It would only be a matter of time, he thought. He took a last bite of his meal, daubed at his mouth with a napkin and lifted his coffee cup for a final swallow.

"More coffee?" she asked, and he marveled at the sound of her voice. It was small and clear and it made him think of fresh running water.

"Yes," he said. "Please."

She got up and headed back for the kitchen, and again he watched with pleasure as she strode across the floor. She was back in a minute with the coffeepot, and she poured his cup full.

"Thank you," he said.

"Uncle?"

"Yes," said Tyson. "Thank you."

She poured his cup full and topped off her own. Then she took the pot back into the kitchen. She returned a moment later and sat down again. Slocum sipped at his coffee, trying to make it last. He was not anxious to get up from this table. He wondered how long it would take for him to get back into her company once he had moved into the bunkhouse. It might take some contriving. Well, he was ready to put his whole mind to it. Yes, sir. It was going to be well worth all the effort. Hell, he told himself, he would kill twenty men and a couple of grizzly bears to get to her. It flashed across his mind that he ought perhaps to be worrying about her uncle, his new employer, Tyson, but he dismissed the thought rather quickly.

"Can I get you anything else, Slocum?" said the sweet thing.

He wanted to ask for something more, but he was full. He was afraid to eat anything else. He had been on the trail with little to eat for a few days, and to eat too much all at once would not be good for him. Reluctantly, he said, "No, thank you. I've had aplenty. It was awful good."

"Thank you," she said. She got up and set about clearing the table.

Tyson pulled out a pocket watch and read it. "We have just about time to catch the boys before they head back to work, Slocum," he said. "Shall we go?"

"Sure," Slocum said, and the two men stood up from the table and excused themselves, Slocum giving Pearlie a final thank-you. They walked to the front door and put on their hats, and Tyson led the way out.

"You can bring along your horse if you'd like to feed him and turn him out in the corral," he said.

They walked down off the porch and Slocum took the reins of the Appaloosa and led him along as they walked toward the bunkhouse and corral. "Mr. Tyson," he said, "I got to tell you that my horse don't hire out."

"Oh?"

"I got in some trouble on a ranch one time. One of the other hands tried to ride him. The boss said that a man's horse hired on with him; anyone could ride it. Well, that don't work too well with my horse. Is that a problem?"

"It shouldn't be. I'll tell Al to inform the crew."

"Thanks," Slocum said.

He put the Appaloosa in the corral, promising to return soon to unsaddle and feed him. Then he walked with Tyson to the cook shack. It was not quite full of cowhands. One man stood up when they walked in. He moved toward them with a quizzical look on his face.

"Shake hands with Slocum, Al," Tyson said. "Slocum, this is Al Chaney, my foreman."

Slocum and Chaney shook hands. Chaney's grip was firm, and his hand was tough from work. The man was about Slocum's size, but he was a younger man. His hair was a light brown, and his eyes were clear blue. He was built firm, and he smiled a friendly smile.

"Glad to know you, Slocum," he said.

"Al," said Tyson, "I've just hired Slocum. He's been riding a long trail, so don't put him to work today. Show him where to bed down and introduce him around. In the morning will be time enough for him to start working. I'll see you later, Slocum. Glad to have you with us."

"Thank you, Mr. Tyson," Slocum said.

Slocum and Chaney watched Tyson walk out the door before they turned to face each other again. Then Chaney called all the cowboys' attention. He introduced each one to Slocum, and Slocum shook their hands. They all seemed friendly enough.

"He starts first thing in the morning," Chaney said. "Right now I'm fixing to show him around a bit. The rest of you can all get on back to work."

As the cowhands made their way out of the cook shack, Chaney turned back toward Slocum. "Have you took care of your horse yet?" he asked.

"Not yet," Slocum said.

"Let's go do that."

Slocum followed Chaney to the corral, where he unsaddled the big Appaloosa. Chaney showed him where he could hang the saddle and tack, and then where to find the oats to give the animal a good meal.

"That's a fine-looking critter you have there," Chaney said.

"Thanks," said Slocum. "Oh yeah. I guess the boss forgot. I told him that no one but me can ride him. He agreed to that all right. Said he'd tell you."

"That won't be no problem," said Chaney. "I'll spread the word. Get your blanket roll and follow me."

Chaney led the way to the bunkhouse and showed Slocum an available bed. Slocum tossed his belongings on top of it. The foreman then took him out behind the bunkhouse and showed him where he could take a bath if he was so inclined. Slocum was. There was a lot of trail dust on him. Chaney then said that he would see Slocum in the morning, and he took his leave. Slocum took a bath and went into the bunkhouse where he put on clean clothes. He asked himself what he would do with the rest of the day, and he thought about Pearlie again. He couldn't hardly just go walking back over to the big house. He'd have to have a good excuse to do that. He stretched out on the bed to consider the matter, and before he knew it, he had fallen into a deep sleep.

He slept soundly until the cowboys all came riding back in for their evening meal. That woke him up. He sat up slowly and rubbed his eyes, yawning. Then he pulled his boots back on, stood up and stretched. Strapping his six-shooter on but leaving his Winchester with the rest of his goods there on the bed, he walked outside. The cowboys were piling into the cook shack. Chaney saw Slocum and walked over to join him. "Come along and have some chow," Chaney said.

"Thanks," said Slocum. "I will."

He couldn't help himself. As they walked toward the cook shack, he shot a glance over at the big house, but he saw no one outside on the porch or the balcony. He sure did want another look at Pearlie. He went on inside the cook shack with Chaney and filled up a plate with grub. It looked and smelled just fine. They sat down and ate. The food was good. Even so, he did not eat too much. It would take him a couple of days to get back his regular appetite.

"You fellows sure have got a good cook here," Slocum said.

The cook was standing not too far away and overheard. "Some of these bastards need to hear that," he said. "Could you say it again a little louder?"

Slocum looked over his shoulder and smiled at the cook.

"I said," he called out loudly, "that you sure have a good cook here."

One skinny cowboy said, "Man, you been out on the trail too damn long."

"Ah, shut up, Boney," said the cook. Everyone laughed. One by one the men began vacating the cook shack. Slocum was not one of the first, but neither did he hang around to be the last to leave. As he walked outside, he glanced again toward the big house, and he saw Al Chaney walking up to the porch. Pearlie stepped out to meet him. As they came together, they embraced, and then Chaney gave Pearlie a kiss on the lips.

"Oh, shit," said Slocum.

**2**

Slocum had a bad night wondering just what the hell he should do. All the anticipated fun of working for Tyson at the Snug T was gone since he had seen the luscious Pearlie in the arms of Al Chaney. Chaney was much a man, and he was a younger man than Slocum. Maybe even better looking. That sure did put a damper on Slocum's plans. Well, hell, they weren't even plans really, just hopes. Anyhow, it took the wind out of his sails and put a hell of crimp in his style. He thought about just riding away first thing in the morning, but then, he was broke. He really did need this job.

He decided that he would grit his teeth and stick it out till payday. With that many good meals under his belt and some pocket money jingling in his jeans, he could ride on off. He could take it till then. He would just have to keep his distance from the big house and try his best not to get even a glimpse of precious Pearlie. It might be tough enough just facing ole Chaney in the mornings, knowing that he was getting into that delicious stuff. He tried to catalog all the things that were wrong with Pearlie, but no matter how hard he wracked his brain, he couldn't come up with a damn thing. At last he got a few hours of troubled sleep.

He was up early the next morning and into the cook shack with the rest of the crew for a good breakfast. This time he ate voraciously. He ate all he could hold and then some more.

He drank several cups of fine coffee for good measure. Then he got his orders from Al Chaney, saddled up his Appaloosa and went to work. The cowhands were all good at their jobs, and Slocum found it easy to work with them. He did his best work, too. Chaney complimented him at the end of the first day, and several of the cowhands started trying to get chummy with him. This was a job he could work at for a long time. It was a comfortable job, and if Slocum had not been so stuck on that girl at the big house, he would have been right comfy in it. But he was trying not to get too complacent in the job. He kept telling himself that he would be leaving come payday.

A week went by. Then after breakfast, Chaney caught up with Slocum at the corral. Slocum was just tightening his cinch on the big Appaloosa.

"Slocum," said Chaney.

"Yeah."

"The boss is going into town this morning. He's got some business at the store. Maybe the bank, too. I ain't sure what all, but I'm going in with him. Charlie Bob and Flank Steak are riding along. Miss Pearlie's going in to do some shopping. I want you to ride in with us."

"You looking for trouble?" Slocum asked.

"We ain't looking for it," said Chaney, "but if it comes along, we aim to be ready. You got the stomach for it?"

"Hell yes," said Slocum, and it came to him just then that he was by God in the mood for a fight. Just let anyone try to start anything with Tyson or any of his crew. He'd clean the bastard's plow in a minute. He finished saddling up his horse and mounted. Riding out of the corral, he noticed Flank Steak driving a buggy up to the big house. Charlie Bob was riding up behind him leading an extra saddle horse. Chaney rode out of the corral behind Slocum. He slowed down to give some orders to a couple of hands. In another couple of minutes, Slocum was beside the buggy. Flank Steak had crawled out and mounted the extra horse that Charlie Bob had brought up. Chaney rode up just as Tyson and Pearlie came out of the house.

As the two came down the stairs, Chaney dismounted and handed the reins of his horse to Tyson. Then he helped Pearlie into the buggy and climbed up behind her to take the reins. "We ready?" he said.

"Let's go," said Tyson, and Chaney flicked the reins. The whole entourage headed toward the main gate. In a minute, Tyson had dropped back to ride along beside Slocum.

"Well, Slocum," he said, "I haven't seen you for a while. How's it going for you?"

"Everything's going just fine, Mr. Tyson," Slocum said.

"No complaints?"

"Not a one."

"Well I'm glad to hear it. I try to run a good outfit here. I believe that Al Chaney is as good a foreman as a ranch ever had. He can be firm, but he's fair."

"He's an easy man to get along with," Slocum said.

"Yes. And the work?"

"I won't say it's a breeze," Slocum said, "but it ain't killing me either."

"Slocum, I don't know what Al said to you this morning, but I feel I should tell you the reason you were asked to come along."

"He said something about being ready for trouble should it come our way," Slocum said.

"Yes. Well, I guess that's about it really. I haven't had any real trouble with LeDoux so far. Just threats and hard looks. One time Flank Steak got into a fistfight with one of LeDoux's hands, but nothing more came of it. But I can't help but think that something could break loose at just about any moment, so when I go into town, I like to have plenty of company. You may have noticed that I don't carry a gun. Generally speaking, I don't believe in them, but I've been convinced that out here, sometimes they're necessary."

"I've found that to be the case," Slocum said.

"Yes. Well, to be frank with you, that's one of the reasons I offered you this job in the first place. If you don't mind my saying so, you have the look of a man who is, shall we say, familiar with firearms?"

"I've had more than a few occasions to put mine to use," Slocum said.

"Let's hope you don't have any such occasion today," said Tyson.

As they pulled into Hangout, Slocum could see a crowd of men around a loaded wagon in the street. As they drew in closer, he could tell that the men were in front of a store. The sign over the door read, "Tyson's." It looked to Slocum as if the trouble had already found them. He glanced over at Tyson. Tyson's jaw tightened, and he kicked his horse in the sides to hurry on in. Slocum kept up with his boss, and Flank Steak and Charlie Bob were right behind. Al Chaney slowed the buggy and stopped it a safe distance from the crowd. He got out and walked up to the scene, leaving Pearlie alone in the buggy. She got out and followed.

"What's going on here, Freddie?" said Tyson.

"I was just about to unload this merchandise, Mr. Tyson," said the man called Freddie, "when LeDoux and his boys came up."

Tyson looked at a large man about fifty years old with an unshaven face. The man had developed a bit of a potbelly, but he was still hard and tough-looking. He wore a six-gun at his left side. His loose britches were held up by gallouses.

"What's it all about, LeDoux?" said Tyson.

"This load of stuff was meant for my store," LeDoux said. "Freddie here is trying to take it over."

"That's not true," Freddie protested.

"This is easy to solve," Tyson said. He turned to the driver of the wagon. "Let's see what your bill of lading says."

"I don't want no part of this," said the driver.

"Just show us the bill," said Tyson.

"We don't need to see no bill," LeDoux said. He pulled some paper money out of his pocket and shoved it into the hand of the driver. "You just go on over to the Bird's Beak and have yourself a drink on me. We'll settle things here."

The driver turned to hurry off toward the saloon, but Slocum stepped quickly in front of him and grabbed him by the lapels. He looked the man hard in the face, and the little man stood still, quaking. Slocum felt the man's pockets and pulled out a piece of paper. He glanced at it quickly, then held it out toward Tyson. "Is this what you want?" he asked.

Tyson took the paper. "Yes," he said. Slocum turned the driver loose, and the frightened man ran for the Bird's Beak as fast as he could go. "You're mistaken, LeDoux," Tyson said. "This bill is clearly for my store. Here. You can see for yourself." He passed the bill to LeDoux. Le Doux took it and, without looking at it, tore it in half and threw it on the ground.

"I don't care what that damn piece of paper says. I know when a load of stuff is meant for me," he said.

"Me and my boys are going to unload this wagon into my store," said Tyson.

"The first one to touch anything in that wagon is going to get a bullet in the belly," LeDoux said.

Tyson opened his coat out wide. "You can see that I'm unarmed," he said. "I'll be the first to touch something." He walked over to the wagon and took hold of a box. One of LeDoux's men pulled out his revolver. Slocum was fast, and his shot tore through the gunman's chest, knocking him flat on his back in the street. The rest of the LeDoux men stopped still, their hands ready to grab gun handles, afraid to move any further. The man on the ground gurgled his last breath. Slocum looked straight at LeDoux, his Colt still out and ready to fire again. LeDoux eyed him hard.

"You've just murdered poor old Wilbur," he said. "Sheriff Comstock will hear about this."

"Your poor old Wilbur slapped leather first," Slocum said. "Go fetch your sheriff."

"I see you've went to hiring on professional gunfighters, Tyson," LeDoux said. "Folks around here ain't going to like that."

"And just what do you call these men who are gathered around you?" Tyson said. "Slocum, here, is just one of my cowhands, and like he said, Wilbur drew first."

"Come on, boys," LeDoux said. "We ain't no match for

professional killers. You ain't heard the last of this, Tyson. You'll be hearing from me."

He turned and stalked off, followed by his gang. Slocum, Tyson and the rest stood and watched them go, all headed for the Bird's Beak. "Well then, let's get it unloaded," Tyson said. Slocum and all the others set to unloading the wagon into the store. They were about halfway through when Slocum noticed a man walking toward them wearing a star on his vest. He was lanky and wore a drooping mustache. Slocum nudged Tyson and nodded toward the man. Tyson stopped what he was doing and looked.

"Sheriff Comstock," he said. "He's a LeDoux man."

Slocum and Tyson stood shoulder to shoulder on the sidewalk, barring the man's way. He walked on up to them and stopped. He glanced into the street where the body of poor old Wilbur still lay. Then he looked Slocum in the face.

"You the man that did this?" he asked.

"Who's asking?" said Slocum.

"My name's Comstock." He tugged at the side of his vest that wore the star. "I'm the sheriff here. Did you kill that man?"

"I did."

"I'll have to take your gun," the sheriff said.

"I don't think so," said Slocum. "If you take my gun, that bunch will come back looking for me. I'd be an easy mark if I was unarmed."

"They won't come looking for you 'cause you'll be in jail."

"Comstock," said Tyson, "everyone saw what happened. Wilbur drew his gun first. There can be no reason to hold Slocum in jail or to disarm him."

"I just talked to a whole bunch of men who seen the whole thing," Comstock said. "They didn't see it like that."

"They wouldn't," said Tyson. "They were all LeDoux men, I'm sure."

"And you're all together here, too," said the sheriff.

"Then it's our word against theirs," Tyson said.

"I don't think so," said Flank Steak, stepping forward.

"There was a mess of folks standing around on the sidewalks just watching. You can ask any of them what they saw."

"I won't have you telling me how to do my job," Comstock said.

"Someone needs to tell you," said Slocum.

"Someone besides LeDoux," Flank Steak said.

"Now see here—" Comstock started, but he was interrupted.

"You see here, Mr. Comstock," said Tyson. "I believe in law and order, but I don't believe that you're a proper representative of it. I believe that you're bought and paid for by LeDoux, and until we have a proper lawman here, I won't have you ramrod any of my men into jail on charges trumped up by LeDoux. Now you can just be on your way. We have work to do here."

"Unloading that wagon?" Comstock said.

"To start with," said Tyson.

"There seems to be some question about the goods in that wagon, too," Comstock said.

Charlie Bob picked up the two pieces of the paper that LeDoux had torn in half and walked over to the sheriff. He held them out. "This here will clear that up right away," he said.

Comstock took the papers and read. "Hmm," he said. "I guess you're right about that. It does have your name on it, Tyson. I reckon you can go on and unload. I still say that Slocum here ought to give me his gun and come on over to the jailhouse with me."

"Not a chance, Sheriff," Slocum said.

Flank Steak came pulling a couple of people up by the arms. They were men who had been standing on the sidewalk when the shooting occurred. He hauled them right up to where Comstock was standing, still facing Slocum and Tyson. "Here, Sheriff," he said. "Here. Talk to these men."

"Who the hell are they?"

"They're witnesses, by God, and they don't work for us and they don't work for LeDoux. Talk to them."

"I seen it all, Sheriff," said one man. "That man laying there in the street, he drawed first."

"You sure?"

"Hell yes."

The other man said, "I seen it, too. He's right about that. No question. This man shot Wilbur after Wilbur had done drawed his gun and was about to shoot Mr. Tyson there. It was plain as day."

"Plain as the nose on your face," said the first man.

Comstock looked at the ground and grumbled. He shuffled his feet. "Well, all right," he said finally. "I guess I got to let you go. For now." He looked up again into Slocum's face. "But you watch your step in my town from here on. You hear me?"

"Sheriff," said Slocum, "I don't like you. From here on, you watch your ass anytime I'm anywhere near. You hear me?"

Comstock turned and walked away. He was headed back toward the Bird's Beak. Slocum stood watching him go, gritting his teeth. He tried to recall if he had ever wanted to shoot a sheriff so badly before this.

"Slocum," said Tyson, "I'm not sure that it was wise of you to threaten the sheriff that way."

"If you want me to quit and move on, Mr. Tyson, I will."

"No," said Tyson. "I don't want that. But I don't want you giving them any more reason than they have already to want to kill you."

"We both should have thought of that before I shot that Wilbur fellow," Slocum said. "Course, if I'd have stopped to think about that, you'd be dead now, wouldn't you?"

"Yes. I believe you're right. Well, let's get this wagon unloaded."

They set back to work. In another minute, Pearlie walked up. She stopped beside Al Chaney, who had just grabbed a sack of flour and rolled it onto his shoulder. But she was looking at the body of Wilbur.

"Al?" she said.

Chaney stopped and looked down at her.

"Are they just going to leave that man lying there in the street?"

# 3

For the next few days things were relatively quiet. Nothing more was heard from LeDoux or from Sheriff Comstock. Slocum was doing his work, and everyone seemed relatively content on the Snug T Ranch. Slocum avoided getting too close to the ranch house, and he saw little of Pearlie. He did not see much more than that of Reginald Tyson. At last he had worked up until his first payday, and he had also earned a couple of days off. He thought about his resolution to quit the job at the first payday, but he hesitated. He could always quit. Besides, he had no place in mind to head for. He saddled up his Appaloosa and rode into Hangout. He planned on making a night of it, so he went straight to the stable and put away his horse. Then he walked down the street to the Bird's Beak. He walked inside and bellied up to the bar. The place was fairly busy, but in a minute, the bartender came over to him.

"What'll it be?" he said.

"A bottle of good bourbon whiskey," Slocum said, "and a glass."

The barkeep put the bottle and glass on the counter, and Slocum paid for the bottle. He picked up the glass and bottle in his left hand and turned to face the big room. He spotted an available table in a far corner and took his whiskey over there to sit down. His back was to the wall. He poured him-

self a drink and downed it fast. Then he poured another. He
sipped the second drink. He had no desire to drink himself
stupid out in public in Hangout. He figured that some of the
cowboys he saw in the place likely worked for LeDoux, and
sure enough, in a few more minutes the man came in. He
was joined immediately by about a half dozen of the men
who had been at the bar. They clustered together around a
big, round table near the bar.

Soon Slocum could see them glance now and then in his
direction. He would pretend not to see them, make out like
he had no idea they were even in the room. Even so, he
managed to keep an eye on them. He had about finished his
second drink when a pretty young painted girl came walking
toward him with a big smile on her face. She walked up and
leaned both hands on the table and looked him in the eyes.

"Hi, stranger," she said. "Would you like some company?"

Slocum did not often bother with prostitutes. He had
never felt the need. But just at that moment, he was feeling
neglected. He'd been thinking again of the pretty Pearlie and
that damned foreman at the Snug T who was bound to be
getting into her britches. He was feeling sorry for himself.

"Sure," he said. "Sit down." She sat in the chair next to
his left arm. "Can I buy you a drink?" he asked.

"I'd love one," she said, and she waved an arm at the
bartender. He brought her a glass, and Slocum poured it full
of whiskey. "Thanks," she said, as she picked it up to take
a sip.

"What do they call you?" Slocum asked.

"Ginger Spice," she said.

"I'll bet you are," he said.

"What?"

"Never mind."

"What do you go by?" she asked.

"I'm Slocum," he said.

"Just—"

"Slocum."

"Okay, Slocum," she said, lifting her glass. "Here's to you."

Ginger Spice had a pretty face and a fetching figure that showed well in her bawdy house clothing. Her hair was dark brown, and her lips were pouty. Her ample breasts were shoved up to their best advantage by the stays in her bodice. Slocum got to thinking, I could do a lot worse. He even liked her.

"I've never seen you in here before," she said.

"I never been in here before."

"New in town?"

"Yeah. Just passing through, but I took a job for a spell out at the Snug T."

"Oh. Reggie's place. He's a nice man."

Slocum thought it was amusing to think about Tyson with this girl. Well, shoot, the man was single, living with his niece. What the hell?

"He seems all right," he said.

"So you're a cowhand?"

"From time to time," Slocum said. "I've done a lot of jobs."

"You like ranch work?"

"Better'n most I've done," he said.

"Where are you from, Slocum?"

"All over. I move around."

He finished his second drink and poured a third. It was about time for him to slow down. He looked at Ginger's drink. She still had half of what he had poured.

"Slocum?" she said.

He gave her a questioning look.

"You want to get out of here? Just you and me?"

"Where would you take me?" he said.

"We have some rooms out back. Real private."

"Let's go," he said. He stood up, taking the bottle and his glass. Ginger stood up and took her glass in her left hand. With her right, she clutched Slocum's left arm. She smiled up at him as they walked through the big room of the Bird's Beak. Slocum noticed the LeDoux crowd eyeing him as they walked by. He tried to appear as if he did not even see them. They walked out the back door, and Slocum saw a row of small clapboard houses. Ginger led him to one of them and opened the door. It was dark inside, and his eyes were not accustomed to it. He couldn't see a damned thing. Ginger let go of his arm and crossed the room to a small table, where she struck a match and lit a lamp.

The room was neat, but it was furnished sparsely. There were hooks on the wall for hanging clothes on. There was a table near the door with a bowl and a pitcher of water on it. A towel was hanging on the wall above the table. Slocum glanced at the door. There was no lock. He crossed the room to get a straight chair which he took back to the door and jammed up under the doorknob.

"No one will bother us in here," Ginger said.

"Just making sure," said Slocum. He thought about LeDoux and his crowd inside the Bird's Beak. He took off his hat and hung it on a peg. Then, unbuckling his gunbelt, he walked to the bed. He took the rig off, rebuckled the belt and hung it over the nearest front bedpost. Then he sat down on the edge of the bed and started to pull off his boots. Ginger moved in front of him, knelt down, and pulled them off for him. Then she stood up and started undressing. All the while, she looked at Slocum with a smile on her pretty face. Slocum stood up and peeled off his own clothes. Then he took hold of her and pulled her close to him, pressing their two naked bodies together, feeling the warmth and softness of hers against his. She looked up into his face, and their lips met and slowly parted. Their tongues probed into each other's mouth, dueling and dancing.

At last Slocum broke loose, getting into the bed and pulling Ginger in after him. She crawled on top of him and pressed her lips against his again, and while they kissed, his hands stroked her back and moved slowly down to her round buttocks. He stroked and he squeezed. One hand finally slipped down low and moved around her upper thigh to find and then to probe the damp bush that it discovered there.

"Um," she said, feeling his fingers dip into her. At about

that same time, she felt something rise up hard between his legs and bounce against her belly. "Oh," she said. She reached down under herself to find it and grip it hard, and it bucked in her hand. She stroked it up and down, back and forth, and Slocum began to hunch. "Where do you want me?" she said. "How do you want it?"

"Just stay where you are," he told her.

She raised herself up a bit and guided the head of the anxious tool into her waiting, wet slit, and then she sat down hard on it, taking it all the way in. She gasped as she felt its length drive into her, and she felt it throb deep inside. The walls of her vagina rippled, contracted, as if they were milking him. He drove upward, jabbing into her, sliding in and out.

"Oh. Oh. Oh," she said.

Then she sat up straight, her hands on his chest, and smiled down at him. Slowly she slid her ass forward on his loins, and then rocked back again. She slid forward again and back again, and then moved faster and faster, panting out loud, sweat dripping off of her face and her nipples, down onto his chest and belly. Her mouth was opened wide as she sucked in air, rocking back and forth faster and faster. Then she stopped and gasped out loud, and her pussy squeezed and rippled again, caressing him in a marvelous and wonderful way.

"Oh, Slocum," she said. "You're wonderful, and you're not even done yet."

He pulled her down to lie against his chest, and then he put his arms around her and rolled both of them over. Now he was on top, and he started to drive in and out hard and fast, pumping with all his might.

"Oh God," she said. "Oh. Yes."

With each stroke, his pelvis slapped against hers, making a sound like a hand against a bare ass. Slap. Slap. Slap. He took a breast in each hand and squeezed as he continued driving into her depths, pounding against her, hammering away with everything he had. She dug her nails into his back and hunched against him with each thrust he made. Her legs wrapped around his torso, and her feet slapped against his ass. "Ahhh," she cried out, and she sounded like some trapped wild animal.

Slocum felt intense pressure building up deep inside himself, and drove harder and faster, and then he felt the explosion and the sudden release, and he spurted into her dark cavern, again and again, and with each spurt, he thrust again, until at last he was spent. He lay down hard on top of her, his slowly wilting rod still deep inside.

"I like the feel of your weight on me," she said.

He lay still until his tool had shriveled and nearly withdrawn itself, and then he pulled the rest of the way out and rolled over to stretch out there beside her on the bed. He sighed a heavy and contented sigh. She raised up and leaned over his face to give him another kiss.

"You're really something, Slocum," she said.

"You ain't bad yourself," he said.

She got up and walked across the room to the table with the water pitcher and poured a bowl full of water. Then she dipped the towel into the bowl and wrung it out. She walked back to the bed and slowly and tenderly washed him off. Then she hung the towel on a footpost of the bed and lay down beside him again. He rolled over onto a side and fondled a breast.

"You want to go again?" she asked him.

"In a minute," he said.

"You'll have to—"

"I know," he said. "I'll have to pay you again. Don't worry about it. I'll take care of it."

"Slocum," she said, anxious to change the subject now that it had been settled, "are you worried about something?"

"Me? I got no worries."

"I was just thinking about the way you jammed that chair against the door and where you hung your gun up real handy-like. That's all."

"Oh, that," he said. "Well, you never know. I suppose I might could have some unexpected visitors. I just like to be ready. That's all."

"You talking about LeDoux and his boys?"

"How'd you know that?"

"I seen the way they was looking at you in there."

"Well, you got it right," he said. "I guess I kind of pissed them off the other day."

"It was you that shot Wilbur, wasn't it?"

"Yeah."

"I thought so."

"You want me to get out of here?" he asked her.

"No. I want you to stay. I didn't like Wilbur anyhow. He was a—Well, I just didn't like him. That's all."

She snuggled closely against Slocum, and he put an arm around her and held her tightly.

"Well," he said, "whatever he was, he ain't that no more."

"They'll come after you, Slocum. One way or another."

"Wilbur pulled his shooter first," Slocum said. "We had witnesses tell that to the sheriff."

"They'll come after you," she said.

"You want another drink?" he asked her.

"Sure," she said. "I'll get it."

She got up from the bed and found the bottle and two glasses and poured them each full. Then she walked back to the bed and handed one to Slocum. He sat up so he could drink, and she got back in the bed beside him. She held up her glass, and Slocum clinked it with his.

"To a damn good fuck," she said.

Slocum laughed. "You can say that again."

They finished their drinks and put the glasses on the floor beside the bed. Slocum pulled Ginger to him again and kissed her. She felt down between his legs and found him ready to go again, just as he'd said he would be. He took her by the waist and turned her, and she was on her hands and knees, and Slocum moved up on his knees behind her. She reached back with her right hand, found his ready cock and guided it into her hole. It was wet and waiting for him. He thrust forward, shoving in all the way, and she gasped with pleasure. Then Slocum started thrusting again. In and out. Her right hand groped his swinging balls, and she found them heavy in their sack and swinging low. He drove in all the way and stopped, taking deep breaths and enjoying the feeling of being in there.

Then he started again, thrusting and driving and pumping. She bounced her ass back against him as he humped, and again the loud slaps sounded in the little room. "Ah, ah, ah," she said, making a noise with each thrust. "Fuck, Slocum. Fuck me. Fuck me hard."

Slocum pounded himself into near exhaustion, and he was still nowhere near ready to come. He had emptied himself not too long ago, and he felt as if he could go on forever. He decided to let Ginger take over again, and he pulled out and fell over onto his back. She swung aboard as if she were mounting a horse, guided him into the right spot again and sucked his tool up inside her with her lively twat. Then she started rocking away.

When they were both done at last, she washed him again. Then she washed herself.

"Slocum," she said, "if you stay all night—"

"What'll it cost me?" he said.

She told him, and he agreed to it. "There's no place else in this town I want to go," he said.

He stayed there, and she stayed with him. They slept soundly side by side, and in the morning, he got up to dress. She woke up sleepy, looked at him smiling. "You leaving?" she asked.

"I think it's about time," he said.

"Slocum," she said, "when you go out—be careful."

# 4

Slocum went out and found a place for breakfast. He ate hearty and lingered over a few extra cups of coffee. He was about ready to head back toward the Snug T when he remembered that he was out of cigars. He had been out for a while. He decided that he might as well give some money right back to old Tyson, so he walked over to Tyson's store. Freddie was busy behind the counter, but he smiled when he looked over his shoulder and recognized Slocum.

"Good morning, Mr. Slocum," he said. "I'll be right with you."

"No hurry," Slocum said. He wandered up and down the aisles, casually looking at the goods displayed there. In another minute, Freddie was out beside him.

"There now," Freddie said. "Can I help you with something?"

"Oh, I just want some cigars," Slocum said.

The two walked back to the counter together, and then Freddie moved around behind it. He showed Slocum where the cigars were displayed on the counter, and Slocum picked out a handful of his favorites. He paid Freddie and tucked the cigars into a pocket. He had opened the front door and was about to go out when he saw the sheriff standing down in the street beside his Appaloosa. He stopped in the doorway.

"Something I can do for you, Comstock?" he said.

"You can drop that gunbelt and come on along with me to the jailhouse," Comstock said.

"What the hell's the charge?"

"Murder."

"What are you talking about?"

"Poor ole Wilbur," the sheriff said. "We found some more witnesses. They all say you drew first. I got a warrant for your arrest right here in my pocket. You going to come along peaceful-like?"

"Be damned if I am," Slocum said. He had started to move on down toward his Appaloosa when he saw a quick movement across the street. He jumped back inside the store just as a rifle bullet smashed the window glass in the front door.

"What the hell?" said Freddie.

"It's that damned Comstock," Slocum said. "He's got some men across the street with rifles."

"What do they want?"

"They want to charge me with Wilbur's murder."

"Again?"

"They got some new witnesses."

"I can imagine how they got them, too," Freddie said. "What are we going to do?"

"Let me see if they'll let you get out of here," Slocum said.

"I don't—"

Slocum did not wait to hear what Freddie was about to say. Instead, he yelled out to the sheriff.

"What do you want, Slocum?" Comstock said. "You ready to give up?"

"I want you to hold your fire while Freddie gets out of here. He's innocent. No sense in getting him hurt."

"I got Freddie there wrote down as accessory. He needs to surrender, too."

"They mean to get both of us, Slocum," Freddie said. He picked up a gun from underneath the counter, opened a box of shells and started loading the weapon.

"Come on out, you two, and you won't get shot," Comstock called out.

"We'll just get hanged is all," Slocum answered, and then he fired a shot that knocked the sheriff's hat off. Comstock scampered for a better hiding place, and several rifles were fired almost at once. Slocum huddled down beneath a window, and Freddie dropped down behind the counter. In another moment the firing slowed down.

"Freddie," Slocum said in a harsh whisper, "can you get out of here the back way?"

"Yeah."

"Can you get to a horse?"

"I think so."

"Well, do it then. Ride out to the ranch as fast as you can, and tell Tyson what's going on here."

"I'll do it," Freddie said, and in a low crouch, he headed for the back door and outside. Slocum raised up carefully for a look outside. He spotted one careless rifleman across the street, and he snapped off a shot that smashed the man's elbow. The man screamed and dropped his rifle, and a barrage of rifle shots were released in Slocum's direction. He tried to figure out how many men were out there, but he couldn't. He wondered how many he would have to kill or hurt before they called off the siege. He'd like to get that fat-assed Comstock, and he promised himself that he would not pass up another chance to shoot the son of a bitch. He eased himself around to a new position and peeked out the window again.

He could have gotten off a shot at another man across the street, but this time, he noticed his Appaloosa standing at the hitch rail right out front. It was a damned miracle that it had not yet been hit by a stray bullet from the sheriff's bunch. He did not want to set them off again if he could help it. He looked at the reins there where he had just draped them casually over the rail. The big horse could easily pull back and run off. Slocum raised up a bit. He fired a shot into the hitch rail, near the horse's head. The big stallion nickered, jerked his head and backed up a few paces. Slocum fired a shot into the ground near its feet, and it ran off down the street, stopping a few doors down, just standing there. It was safely out of the line of fire.

"What the hell's that crazy bastard doing?" a rifleman said.

"Looks to me like he was just getting his horse safe out of the way," said Comstock. "That's real touching."

"Yeah?" the rifleman said. He straightened up and took aim at the unsuspecting horse, but Slocum saw what the man was about to do and snapped off a shot that caught the man in the neck. The man screamed, and his scream turned to a gargling sound as blood spurted from the gaping wound. He fell back against the wall and slid down to a sitting position.

"Don't anyone shoot that horse," Comstock said. "Hell, I want it for myself."

Slocum tried to locate Comstock, but the man was too well hidden. All the riflemen were well hidden, too. He had fired five shots, so he reloaded five more bullets. He watched carefully out the window. Suddenly a man scampered from his hiding place, apparently looking for a better position. Slocum sent a shot into the man's leg. The man screamed and clutched at his wounded leg as he stumbled, sprawling in the dirt of the street. Another man raced out from his cover to help the wounded man to safety. Slocum thought about shooting that one as well but decided against it. One wounded man had two of them out of commission, at least for the moment.

Slocum took advantage of the lull in the action to run back behind the counter for a rifle. He stuffed the pockets of his vest full of boxes of ammunition and moved back to the window while loading the rifle. It was a Winchester, much like his own, and it took the same shells as did his Colt .45. Back at the window with a fully loaded Colt in his holster and a loaded Winchester in his hands, he looked out again. A rifleman across the way had decided to do the same just at the same time. Slocum raised the Winchester and fired a shot that broke the man's shoulder. Everyone on the other side started sending shots into the store. Slocum dropped down low on the floor as cans and bottles and boxes were hit all around him.

He wondered if he could get out the back door, run down the alley and then make it to his horse, mount up and ride out of town without getting hit. It sure did seem like a long shot. Apparently Freddie had gotten away all right. He had not heard any shots right after Freddie's escape. Maybe getting out the back door was the thing to try. He raised up and fired several random shots just to get their attention, and then, as they fired back wildly, he crawled to the back door. He opened it slowly and peered out. There did not seem to be anyone posted out there. That was stupid, he thought, but he was grateful for their stupidity. He slipped out and moved along the back walls of the buildings. He heard the firing stop.

He had made it about as far as he thought he had to go, and he ducked between the buildings there to get back to the street. Reaching the front of the building he was next to, he pressed his back against the wall and peered around the corner. There was his horse standing almost in the middle of the road. He was about to make a run for it, when he heard the sheriff issue an order.

"Burn the damn place down, boys. He'll have to either come out or get himself roasted."

"Hey, Sheriff," one of the boys said, "ain't there a back door?"

"Get around there and watch it," Comstock ordered. The other man made a dash across the street and disappeared.

Soon men appeared on the sidewalk with rags in their hands. They hurried across the street to Tyson's store. Slocum watched as they set the rags on fire and tossed them in through the broken windows. He would never have a better chance. Everyone was watching the flames build up. They were fascinated at watching the store being destroyed by fire and even more fascinated at the thought the fire might be about to roast a man, or two men, alive. Slocum wanted to kill a few more of them, but he knew that his best chance was to just get the hell out of town as fast as he could. He ducked low and ran for the Appaloosa. Mounting quickly, he kicked the horse in the sides and headed out of town. He looked back over his shoulder, and he was not too surprised to note that no one seemed to be looking in his direction.

Comstock and what was left of his riflemen all strolled out into the middle of the street, eyes glued to the flames that grew and consumed what had been Tyson's store. LeDoux appeared from somewhere and walked up to stand beside Comstock.

"Far as we know," Comstock said, "both of them are still in there."

"Could they have got out the back door?" LeDoux asked.

"I sent a man back there to watch," the sheriff said.

They stood in silence for another few minutes, watching as the roof collapsed. The flames grew dangerously close to the buildings just next door on either side, and a bucket brigade was formed to wet down the endangered buildings and try to quench the flames of the two side walls. LeDoux and Comstock stood there until the flames were gone. There was nothing but a pile of smoldering black ash. The buildings on either side had been saved. LeDoux walked up close to the rubble and looked down at it.

"Get some men sifting through this mess," he said. "See if they can find any evidence of the bodies."

He turned and walked back across the street. Comstock called out the names of three men. They came running up to him for their instructions.

"Go on over to LeDoux's store," Comstock said. "Pick up some rakes. I want you to hunt through this ash heap for them two."

When Slocum rode up to the Tyson ranch house, the cowboys had just saddled up horses and everyone was about to mount up and ride. When Tyson saw Slocum coming, he called a halt. Slocum rode up and dismounted.

"They burned your store," he said.

"Thank God you got out safely. When Freddie showed up and told us what was happening, we were afraid that we might not make it in fast enough to save you."

"I appreciate your plans," Slocum said, "but there ain't no hurry now. And that Comstock has got a small army of riflemen all gathered up together. He'd be ready for you if you was to ride on in now."

"Yes, well, I guess we had better change our plans," Tyson said.

"We're going to have to do something, Mr. Tyson," Chaney said. "We can't let LeDoux get away with this. He's declared open war."

Tyson shook his head and walked away from Chaney. Then he walked back. "We can't let ourselves be drawn into a range war, Al," he said. "We can't take the law into our own hands."

"Well, LeDoux has it in his own hands," Chaney said.

"Or maybe in his pocket," said Slocum. "When Comstock had that fire started, he thought that me and ole Freddie was both still in there. He meant to burn us to death."

"That's horrible," said Pearlie, and Slocum realized that he had not even noticed her standing there until that moment. "Comstock is no lawman. He's just another of LeDoux's paid killers."

"You're right, of course," said Tyson. "Even so, that's no reason for us to start acting the same way."

"What else can we do?" said Chaney.

"I can send a wire to the governor," said Tyson. "I can ask him to send us a real lawman."

"Old Chormley down at the telegraph office would take the wire straight over to LeDoux," Chaney said. "The governor would never see it."

"Yes, well, you're probably right about that," Tyson said. "I'll just have to ride over to Farleyville to send the wire. LeDoux doesn't have any men over there."

"That might work all right," Chaney said.

"Of course it will," said Tyson. "Al, put my horse away for now, but have him ready to ride first thing in the morning."

"I'll have several horses ready in the morning."

"No. Just mine. And Slocum's. We'll make it all right."

"It's a few hours on the other side of Hangout," said Chaney. "I'd say it's about a three-hour ride."

"We'll have to swing wide around the town," Slocum said.

"Yes. We can take the mountain trail to the west," said Tyson. "It will slow us down a bit, but we'll avoid Hangout all right. Well now, Al, you can get the boys all back to work. Everything's settled for now."

"All right, Mr. Tyson."

"Slocum," said Tyson. "I suspect you could use a drink. Come on up on the porch and sit with me."

"Yeah," said Slocum. "I could use one."

"Or two?"

The two men walked up onto the porch, and Slocum sat down while Tyson went into the house for a bottle and two glasses. He was back out in a minute and poured the two glasses nearly full, handing one to Slocum. Then he sat down and put the bottle on a table that stood between the two chairs. He lifted his glass and said, "Cheers." Slocum didn't quite think the toast was appropriate, but he lifted his glass. Then he took a long swallow.

"Thanks," he said. "It ain't every day I just escape being cooked alive."

"Yes. I daresay. I'm sorry for that, Slocum. I didn't really think that we were that near open warfare when I offered you a job. If you like, you can ride off from here with no hard feelings."

"That's a tempting offer, Mr. Tyson, but I ain't never run from a fight before, and I don't think I'll start now. Besides, those fellows have made me mad now."

Tyson smiled. "I'm glad to hear you say that. The governor knows me. I think he'll respond to my request all right. We'll get this thing settled, and we'll put LeDoux and his gang behind bars where they belong. I don't think there'll be need for any more fighting."

"I hope you're right about that, Mr. Tyson."

But Slocum had seen range wars build up before. This

one was ready to burst wide open. And he had not seen a distant government react swiftly to a needful situation. He did not hold out the same hope that Tyson did. He sipped his whiskey. It was good. He wondered if he would have the luxury of sipping many more in this life.

# 5

Early the next morning Slocum and Tyson rode toward
Hangout. As Slocum understood it, they would turn off the
road a few miles before reaching the town and go up into
the mountains on an old and little used trail. That would take
them around Hangout. Then they would ride down again to
the main road, thus avoiding any chance of running into
LeDoux, his crooked sheriff or any of their gang. Back at
the ranch, Al Chaney was charged with getting the herd
ready to drive to the Army fort, a two-day trip. Tyson was
sure that he would get the contract. He talked about it with
Slocum as they rode along.

"Maybe that's what caused ole LeDoux to go into action
when he did," Slocum said.

"Hmm," mused Tyson. "You could be right about that."

"I reckon it's for quite a bit of money," Slocum said.

"Yes," said Tyson. "Considerable."

"That'll do it almost every time."

The road began to drop off sharply to their right. The
closer they came to the turn off to the mountain trail, the
steeper the drop-off grew. It became a rocky shelf falling
down to a swift-moving stream. Slocum was studying the lay
of the land there when Tyson spoke up abruptly.

"Hello?" said Tyson. "What's this?"

Slocum looked. Up ahead the road was blocked by seven

men. They all had weapons drawn and cocked. Sitting horseback dead center of the group was Sheriff Comstock. Slocum pulled back on his reins.

"Hold up," he said. "We might have to run from this one."

"No. I don't think so," Tyson said. "I'll ride ahead and talk to them. See what they want."

"Don't be a fool, Tyson," said Slocum. "I can tell what they want just by looking."

"You can't be too sure, Slocum."

Tyson nudged his horse forward at a slow pace. Slocum hesitated. If the men started to shoot, there would be little he could do. He might get one or two of them. He decided that if that happened, he'd be sure to get Comstock first.

"Tyson," he said, "let's back off of this."

"Just let me talk to them first," Tyson said, and suddenly a barrage of shots rang out from the seven men. All of them were firing. A shot grazed Slocum's head, and he went dizzy. The big Appaloosa screamed and reared, and Slocum lost his saddle. He fell off to the right and slipped over the edge. He tried to grab hold of something, anything, but his grip failed. He slid. Then he banged into a rock ledge, and he nearly blacked out. Groaning, he rolled over. He heard the shots continuing above. He reached for his Colt, but he did not have the strength to haul it out. The shooting stopped, and he heard the sound of riders coming close. Then the riding stopped.

"Is he dead?" said someone.

"Make sure," said Comstock.

There were a dozen more shots. Slocum struggled to get up. He couldn't manage. Then he heard someone say, "What about that other one?"

"That Slocum?" said Comstock. "He went over the edge. Check on him."

He heard some footsteps come close to the edge above him. He managed to slip the Colt out of the holster and was about to thumb back the hammer, or try to, when he realized that he was underneath the ledge on another shelf. He could not see up there. They could not see him either. He wondered

if they would try to climb down to see if he was dead or
alive.

"I don't see nothing, Comstock."

There were more footsteps, and then Slocum heard the
sheriff's voice again.

"He might have fell on in that stream and been swept
away," he said.

"He might not be dead."

"I seen him hit in the head," said the sheriff, "and I seen
him go over. If he survived that, he won't be worth much. I
ain't going to try to climb down this son of a bitch to see
about him. If any of you boys wants to, that's your business."

"Well, hell, if you don't care, I don't neither."

In another minute or so, Slocum heard the horses ride off.
Again, he tried to get up. Instead, he fell back and the world
went black.

Slocum came to and found that it was dark. He had been out
cold all the day long. His head was throbbing like blazes,
but he did manage to get up and out from under the shelf.
He did not have much room on the ledge after that, but he
could stand up. He tried to study the rock face above him,
but it was hard to tell anything in the darkness. Even so, he
had no intention of spending the night on this ledge. The
night air was already beginning to cool off. It would be
downright cold pretty soon. He checked his Colt to make
sure it was still holstered at his side, and then he reached up
to feel around on the rocks.

He found a good handhold and places to put his feet. The
problem was that he could not tell what was above them. He
just might get himself up a ways and get stuck. That was not
a pleasing prospect in the dark. Still, he had to try it. He got
a good, firm grip, then felt with his foot for a step. He heaved
himself up. His head pounded. He reached around with one
hand until he found another spot. Each move of a hand and
each move of a foot was a feeling job. One time, the rock
he had gripped with his right hand broke loose. He gripped
all the tighter with his left and listened as the rock fell,

bouncing against the wall and finally splashing into the water below. He moved up slowly, until at last he found a bush growing out of the rock. He grasped a branch and pulled at it, testing it. It seemed to have a solid hold. He decided to take a chance, and he grabbed it with both hands and heaved himself up. The bush held.

He found himself back up on top, and he got both his arms onto the road and wriggled the rest of the way, rolling over onto his back as he crawled up. He lay there breathing heavily. His head was still throbbing. He closed his eyes, and then he realized that he could easily have gone back to sleep, if it was sleep. He might have been passed out. He might pass out again. He was tempted to do that, but something told him not to give in to it. He opened his eyes. With a major effort, he got up to his feet. He looked up and down the road. He could see no horses. He wondered if his Appaloosa had run off, or if the sheriff had managed to capture it.

Then he saw the body just a few feet away lying in the middle of the road. It was Tyson. There was no doubt about it. The fool. The damned fool. He had wanted the world to operate according to law, according to a set of decent rules, but the rules around Hangout were not decent ones. They were kill or be killed. And Tyson, the innocent, had been killed. Slocum staggered over to the body. Even in the darkness he could tell that it had been shot to pieces. And the man wasn't even wearing a gun. Again, Slocum looked up and down the road. Again, he saw no sign of a horse.

He would have to walk back to the ranch. He didn't know if he could make it, but he had to try. And there was no way he could take Tyson's body with him. He couldn't bring himself to just let it lay there in the road like that. He dragged it to the side of the road and laid it out straight. Then he covered it with rocks as gently as he could to protect it from scavengers. It was only temporary. He knew that Pearlie would want to recover the body.

He did the best he could under the circumstances and then he started to walk back toward the Snug T. It was going to be a long walk. He thought about the clear, running water down below. He would sure like to dunk his head into that stream, but he knew better than to try to get down to it in the dark. He tried to remember if there was some place on down the road where the stream was accessible, but he couldn't recall anywhere. He did not think the stream ran alongside the road, not until the road was well up above. Then it came in from some other direction. Even a canteen of water would have helped. He couldn't get himself to stop thinking about water.

He staggered along, one step at a time. To get his mind off of water, he started to think about Sheriff Comstock and how good it was going to feel when he could get the fat son of a bitch in his gunsights. The same for LeDoux, but Comstock was the main one in Slocum's mind. Then he thought about the other six men who had been along with Comstock when they killed poor Tyson. In his mind, he called up their faces one at a time. He did not want to forget any one of them. He meant to kill them all. And he would do it face to face. Each man would know who was about to kill him, and he would know why he was about to be killed. Slocum had seen men ambushed, murdered, before, but he could not recall such a brutal and unwarranted killing as this one. He realized he had developed a deep hatred for LeDoux and everyone associated with him. He determined to nurture that hatred until he had gotten every one of them.

His foot kicked a rock, and he stumbled and fell hard, barely catching himself just before his face would have smashed into the road. He was exhausted. He wanted to roll over and go to sleep. His head was still throbbing with pain. He wondered whose bullet had grazed him, and he wondered how deep the crease in his skull was. He reached a hand up to feel the wound, but all he could feel was a mass of nasty dried blood caked in his hair. He forced himself back to his feet and started walking again.

He walked the night away, and the sun began peeking out over the far eastern horizon. Slocum was staggering all over the road, lurching from one side to the other. If anyone had happened along, they would have thought him drunk. He told himself that he couldn't stop to rest. It was the walking, the continuing to move, that was keeping him alive. His feet and legs were hurting him though. If he could just rest them a little while, he should be able to go on to the ranch. He was afraid to lie down though. At last he spotted a low, somewhat flat rock by the side of the road. He walked over to it and sat down. There was nothing to lean back on. He sat there, sitting up straight, relieving his legs and feet.

He wondered if someone from the ranch would be along soon, and then he realized that they would think that he and Tyson were still in Farleyville. No. He changed his mind. Farleyville was only about a three-hour ride. They would have gotten there by noon, maybe had some lunch, sent the wire and been back at the Snug T by suppertime. They ought to be getting worried at the ranch about this time. Slocum heaved himself back up to his feet and started to walk again. He and Tyson should have been home last night before dark. If Chaney had figured that out, he would have known that it would not have made any sense to go out after them late last night. He would have waited until morning to get started riding. It was still early. Maybe they'd come along before too much more time had passed.

By the time Al Chaney, Flank Steak and Charlie Bob came riding down the road, leading two extra horses, Slocum was practically walking in his sleep. He walked right past them. He did not even see them, did not hear the horses' hooves, or the words of the men as they called out to him.

"Slocum," said Chaney. "Slocum. What the hell are you doing?"

The three men halted their mounts, and Al Chaney jumped out of the saddle. Slocum was still walking ahead. Chaney ran after him and grabbed him around the shoulders. Slocum tried to walk on.

"Slocum, damn it. Stop."

Charlie Bob ran up to join Chaney, and together they wrestled Slocum to the ground. Chaney cradled Slocum's head in his lap. "Get some water, Flank Steak," he said.

"Water," said Slocum. His eyes were opened, but they did

not focus on Chaney or anything else. They stared out like the eyes of a dead man. Flank Steak ran up with a canteen. He had already pulled the cork. He handed it to Chaney. Chaney poured some onto Slocum lips, and Slocum started to lick his lips. Chaney put the canteen to his mouth, and Slocum drank. Chaney pulled it away before Slocum could guzzle too much. Then he pulled a bandana out of his pocket and poured water over it. He mopped Slocum's face, and he daubed a bit at the matted blood in Slocum hair. Slowly, Slocum came around. His eyes began to focus. He looked up.

"Chaney?" he said.

"Yeah, Slocum. It's Al Chaney."

"Al Chaney," said Slocum.

"Flank Steak and Charlie Bob are with me. When you and Tyson didn't come back last night, we begun to worry about you."

"They killed him," said Slocum. "Murdering bastards. Shot him down like a mad dog."

"Mr. Tyson's dead?" said Flank Steak.

"Back down the road there," said Slocum. "I covered him up as best I could. They shot him to pieces."

"Who done it, Slocum?" Chaney asked.

"Comstock. Six others. I don't know their names, but I know their faces."

"Slocum," said Chaney, "do you think you can ride?"

"A hell of a lot easier than I can walk."

"Come on. Let's get you mounted."

They helped Slocum to his feet and then into the saddle of one of the two extra horses they had brought along.

"Can you take us back to Mr. Tyson?" Chaney asked.

"Yeah," Slocum said. "It ain't far. I walked from there to here overnight."

Back down the road, they found the body and uncovered it.

"Holy Jesus," said Charlie Bob when he saw the wounds. They wrapped the body in a blanket and then tied it on the other extra horse. Then they turned around and headed back for the Snug T.

"Pearlie's going to take this hard," Chaney said.

"We've got to do something about this," said Flank Steak.

"We'll do something, all right," Chaney said.

Slocum recovered a bit, and as they rode along, he told them what had happened.

"I should have made him turn around," he said.

"Don't blame yourself, Slocum," said Chaney. "I know how damn stubborn the boss could be."

"He was a good man," said Charlie Bob.

"The best," said Flank Steak. "The best I ever worked for."

"We get the boss proper buried," said Chaney, "and get Slocum doctored and put to bed, we'll get the boys and take us a ride into town. We'll wipe out that whole mess of coyotes once and for all."

"No," Slocum said.

"What?"

"Not in town. They'll be barricaded up in there. They'll be expecting us now after what they did. Besides, I ain't going to bed. I'm going after the sons of bitches with you."

"You don't have to do that, Slocum," Chaney said.

"Besides," said Charlie Bob, "you ain't in no shape to go out riding and shooting and all."

"I can outdraw and outshoot anyone of you," Slocum said. "Give me a little time to rest up. Give me a meal, and I'll be ready to go."

"You didn't even know the boss all that long," said Chaney. "What's got you so riled up?"

"I liked him," said Slocum. "And I don't like being shoved around."

# 6

Down the road a few miles, they came across Slocum's big stallion. It had once again managed to escape the clutches of Sheriff Comstock. Slocum was glad to see the animal, and he got off the borrowed ranch horse and mounted his Appaloosa right away. The rest of the ride back to the Snug T rested Slocum's bones and muscles some. They informed Pearlie of what had happened to her uncle, and while she mourned in private, Slocum cleaned himself up and put on fresh clothes. He left the bunkhouse to find Al Chaney gathering up almost all of the cowhands there in front of the big ranch house. Taking his horse out of the corral, he hurried over to join them.

"I thought I told you to get some rest," Chaney said.

"I'm all right," said Slocum.

Just then, Pearlie came out of the house. She had washed her face, but it still showed that she had been crying. She walked to the front of the porch and stood tall. "Al," she called out. Chaney turned to face her. "What are you doing?"

"We're going after Comstock and LeDoux, Pearlie. There's no other way to get any justice around here."

"Just hold on a minute," she said. "Listen to me. Comstock is sheriff because LeDoux put him in there. No other reason."

"That's just my point," said Chaney.

"Then let's do the same thing he did."

"What are you talking about?"

"Let's elect a constable and issue warrants for the arrest of all of those men."

"They won't buy that," said Chaney.

"I don't care if they buy it or not," said Pearlie. "You can kill them when they resist arrest. But if anyone comes in here when it's all over, we can always tell them that it was legal."

"But how are we going to do it?"

"We'll do it right here today," she said. "Send some of the boys out to our neighbors we know will go along with us. Get them over here in a hurry. We'll have us an election."

It took a few hours, but by mid-afternoon, there were enough men present at the Snug T to make a respectable-sized crowd for such goings-on. They all gathered there in front of the house. Up on the porch, Pearlie had a table set up with a wooden box on top. She had cut up pieces of paper and had a few pencils on the table alongside the papers. When she decided that there were enough voters, she called for order.

"We're here to elect a constable," she said, "who will go after LeDoux and Comstock and their whole bunch of out-laws. I guess most of you know by now that they murdered my uncle yesterday. You all know that he never carried a gun. They shot him down in cold blood. They would have killed Slocum, too, had he not fallen off the road. They thought that he was dead. Now let's get down to business."

"Who will we elect, Pearlie?" called out an elderly rancher close to the front of the crowd.

"I nominate Al Chaney," Pearlie said.

The crowd cheered. When they calmed down some, Pearlie went on.

"Are there any more nominations?"

Some of the folks murmured to one another, but no one spoke up.

"This is a democratic process," Pearlie said. "Anyone here can put forth a nomination."

She waited a respectable moment before continuing.

"I got some ballots all ready up here," she said, "but if there aren't any more nominations, I don't guess we need them. All in favor of Al Chaney for constable say aye."

The crowd roared, "Aye."

Pearlie motioned for Chaney to step up on the porch, and he did. He motioned for quiet, and when the noise had subsided, he spoke to the gathering. He was brief and to the point.

"I appreciate your confidence in me," he said. "Now none of you have to ride with me. There will be no hard feelings. But anyone who wants to ride with me and has his own horse and gun and ammunition is hereby deputized. The rest of you can go on about your business."

Pearlie stepped out again. "Not yet," she said. "We got to keep this legal. I'd like everyone who voted for Al to step up here on the porch and sign his name. I guess that's all of you."

Slocum went up to stand beside Chaney. "I hope you ain't still planning on riding into town," he said.

"Why not?" said Chaney.

"On account of what I said before. They'll be waiting in there. Ready for you. Not only that, but there's lots of innocent folks in town. Someone who don't need to be might get hurt."

Chaney scratched his head. "What do you suggest?"

"LeDoux's got a ranch, don't he?"

"Yeah."

"Why not start there?"

"That's an idea, all right."

"One more thing," said Slocum. "It looks to me like all of the boys is planning on riding with you."

"Looks like it," Chaney said.

"Well, don't take them all. Some has got to stay here and watch the ranch. There ain't no telling what them bastards will try to pull off now that they've done started the killing."

"You're right about that, Slocum," Chaney said. "I'll tell the boys."

Two of the neighbors wanted to ride along, and Chaney

agreed to take them. He selected ten of the Snug T hands, making a posse of fourteen counting himself and Slocum. The rest of the Snug T hands were told to stay on the ranch and watch for any trouble from LeDoux's bunch. "We can't have Pearlie caught here all by herself, now can we?" he said.

"No, Boss," said Flank Steak. "We sure can't have that. We'll watch the place like a hawk. I promise you."

It was nearly suppertime when the posse finally rode out from the Snug T. Slocum rode alongside Chaney. They headed straight for LeDoux's ranch. There was no talking along the way. A grim-faced bunch of riders rode looking straight ahead. They trotted their horses, anxious to get to their destination, but not wanting to wear the animals out. At last they rode onto LeDoux's place. Fourteen horses make a racket, and by the time they reached the ranch house, there were four armed men on the porch. The posse pulled up close to the house.

"What do you want?" called out one of the men.

"We're looking for LeDoux," said Chaney.

"Well, he ain't here. I reckon he's still in town."

"You expecting him back?" Chaney asked.

The man shrugged and grinned. "He comes and goes as he pleases," he said.

Chaney looked at Slocum. "You recognize anyone?" he asked.

"Those two," Slocum said, pointing to the two men on the far right. "They were there. They helped kill Mr. Tyson."

"Shiner and Pitts," said Chaney. "You two come along with us. You're under arrest for the murder of Mr. Tyson."

"Arrest?" said the one called Shiner. "You got no authority to arrest us. Besides, old Tyson got hisself killed resisting arrest. We was part of a posse led by Sheriff Comstock."

"Is that right?" Chaney said. "Well, we just had ourselves an election, and I was elected constable. This is a legal posse with me here. Are you coming along peaceful?"

Shiner and Pitts looked at each other. They looked over

at the other two men beside them there on the porch. The man nearest them said, "Go along with them, boys. They can't get away with this. We'll go after Comstock. He'll take care of it."

"What if they mean to just kill us?" Pitts said.

The man stepped forward. His thumbs were hooked in his gunbelt. "What do you intend to do with these men— Constable?" he said.

"We'll hold them for a trial," said Chaney. "Obviously, we can't keep them in the jail at Hangout. They'll be held in custody at the Snug T for now."

"Do you believe that, Patton?" said Shiner.

Patton spoke to Shiner and Pitts in a low voice. "I ain't got much choice right now, have I? They got us outnumbered here. Most of the boys is in town with LeDoux. I'd say for right now just go along with them. Likely they mean what they're saying. Like I told you, we'll get Comstock, and he'll take care of it."

"Well, Shiner, Pitts," said Chaney. "What'll it be?"

"We'll come along," said Shiner, and he took a step forward.

"Hold it," said Chaney.

Shiner stopped.

"Drop off that gunbelt," Chaney ordered. Shiner hesitated, then unbuckled the belt and let it drop. Pitts did the same thing. "Now, you, Patton, get a couple of saddled horses for these two."

In a matter of a few minutes, the posse, with its two prisoners, was riding back toward the Snug T. There had been no gunfight. The excitement that had been anticipated had not materialized. Yet they felt good. Their first mission had been a success. They had two of the murderers captured. It had been easy. Slocum was not feeling puffed up with pride, however. He had sworn to kill all of the men in the gang that had murdered Tyson. He was not sure now just how that could happen. He wondered if he could just wait and watch them hang. Would it be the same? He did not think so. He had promised himself, and he had promised the murdered man.

Riding back toward the Snug T, they did not move so quickly. They walked the horses. There was no need for any more of a hurry than that. Slocum allowed himself to drop back a little. He rode behind Chaney. The two prisoners, unarmed, but not tied, rode beside the new constable.

"Chaney," said Pitts, "you know this ain't going to work, don't you? You can't just get a bunch of folks together and have a goddamned election whenever you please. It's got to come up legal and on time. It's got to be done by the county government. Comstock's going to make you turn us loose. You know that, don't you?"

"Comstock will have a fight on his hands if he tries that," said Chaney.

"Comstock's the sheriff," said Shiner. "We was part of a legal posse. We told you that."

"Your posse didn't act very legal," Chaney said.

"We had a warrant for Tyson," Pitts said. "He resisted arrest."

"You know as well as I do that's a lie," said Chaney. "Tyson never carried a gun. The only way he could resist was by running, and he was shot from the front, and he was shot to pieces. I never seen a more brutal killing. You boys are going to hang, and that's all there is to it."

Shiner and Pitts gave looks to each other, and they were seen by Slocum. They had just been convinced by Chaney that they had no real hope of surviving if they were taken to the Snug T Ranch. They were desperate men. Slocum noticed Shiner give a slight jerk of the head to Pitts, and Pitts returned a nod. Then suddenly he reached over and jerked the revolver out of Chaney's holster. Slocum moved quickly, going for his own Colt, but Pitts had a good start on him. Pitts's shot rang out first, and the bullet nipped Chaney's ear, as Chaney dodged just in the nick of time. Pitts gave a violent jerk, then slumped over his horse's neck. He slid slowly down to the ground, landing with his head in the water of the cool stream. A few bubbles rose to the surface from his last gurgling breath.

Shiner, still unarmed, jerked his horse around to make a run for it. Just for good measure, Slocum fired a shot into his chest. The horse ran on, Shiney bouncing foolishly in the saddle. At last he fell to the ground, and just a little later, the horse slowed down, then stopped. Chaney was leaning over in his saddle, holding onto his hurt ear, with blood running down his arm.

"Damn," he said.

Charlie Bob, who was already dismounted, ran to Chaney's side.

"Al," he said, "you all right?"

"Ah, shit, I guess so. It's just my damned ear. That's all."

"Slocum got both of the bastards," Charlie Bob said. He pulled the bandana from around his neck and knelt to dip it in the cool water. He squeezed it out a little, then handed it up to Chaney. "Here, Al," he said.

Chaney took the rag and slapped it to his ear. He moaned a little more. Then he said, "What did you say, Charlie Bob?"

"What?"

"You said Slocum got them both?"

"Yeah. That's right."

"But Shiner was unarmed," Chaney said.

"Well, yeah."

"Damn it. Slocum."

"I'm right here, Al," said Slocum. He was still in the saddle, and he was reloading two bullets into the chamber of his Colt revolver.

"Slocum, did you know that Shiner was unarmed?"

"I didn't think too much about it," Slocum said.

"There wasn't no sense in killing an unarmed man."

"That's what I thought about the way they killed Mr. Tyson," Slocum said.

"But we're the law."

"So were they."

"Aw, Al," Charlie Bob said, "it don't make no difference. Both of them deserved to die anyhow. What difference does it make if it was here and now or later? We all know we was going to kill them both."

"But we promised them a trial," said Chaney.

"I never promised them a damn thing," Slocum said.

"Besides, Al, they was trying to kill you," Charlie Bob said.

"Just one of them had a gun," said Chaney.

"Yeah," said Slocum. "Yours."

"All right. So I let the son of a bitch get my gun. It don't bother me that you killed Pitts, but you didn't have to kill Shiner."

"He was running away, Al," said Charlie Bob.

"Killed while trying to escape?" said Chaney.

"Sure as hell," said Charlie Bob.

"All right then," said Chaney. "That's the way we'll tell it."

"Tell it any damn way you want to," said Slocum. "I don't give a shit."

# 7

Slocum rode into Hangout with the constable's posse and the two bodies. They took them straight to the undertaker's establishment. Soon LeDoux and Comstock and a small gang of their followers were there to find out what had happened.

"You might as well know right now, LeDoux," said Chaney, "that we held an election. I was elected constable. We arrested these two men and were going to bring them to trial."

"Arrested them for what?" demanded LeDoux.

"For the murder of Mr. Tyson. Slocum was a witness to the killing."

"Tyson was under arrest himself," said Comstock. "That was a legal posse."

"They didn't act legal," said Slocum. "They murdered an unarmed man with no reason. They shot him full of holes. Enough to kill five men."

"We just have your word for that, now, don't we?" said Comstock.

"There were plenty of people who saw the body," Chaney said. "And everyone knows that Tyson never carried a gun. You admit that you had him under arrest. That's plenty of evidence for holding men for trial."

"But you didn't hold them," Comstock said. "You killed them."

"Murdered," said LeDoux.

"They grabbed my gun and made a break for it," Chaney said. "They were killed trying to escape."

"That's a likely story," said LeDoux.

"At least as likely as yours about the way Mr. Tyson was killed," Slocum said.

"You men are not a legal posse," Comstock said. "I'm the law around here. Legally elected and sworn in. You can't just get a bunch of cowboys together and call it an election. That ain't legal."

"Comstock," said LeDoux, "arrest these men for murder."

"You'll pay hell," said Slocum.

"I have a warrant for the arrest of Comstock," said Chaney.

"Just try to serve it," LeDoux said.

"Let's get it on," Slocum said.

"That's not the way to do it," said Chaney. "We'll get our chance."

"Yeah?" said LeDoux. "Well, we'll be ready for you."

"I'm ready right now," Slocum said. He was staring at Comstock. He had also looked over the gang and spotted two more men he recognized as members of the gang that had murdered Tyson. He was itching to kill them. But Chaney was probably right. If a big gunfight started, some innocent people might be hurt, maybe killed. Slocum decided that he would bide his time unless one of the LeDoux bunch made a move. He wished they would.

It didn't happen though. LeDoux and Comstock and their crowd backed away. They all headed for the Bird's Beak Saloon, some of them looking back over their shoulders as they walked, giving hard looks to Slocum, Chaney and the others. Slocum felt his gun hand twitching.

"Let's get back to the ranch," Chaney said.

The Snug T men all mounted their horses and rode out of town.

It was late that same night when a gang of LeDoux's men, headed by a stocky, scar-faced man wearing two guns, rode out to the Snug T. They did not go close to the ranch house.

They headed for the cattle on a far pasture. Close to the milling herd, the scar-faced man held up a hand, and they all stopped.

"Homer," said the scar-faced man, "do you see them two cowboys with the herd over there?"

"I see them, Jules," said Homer.

"Can you hit them from here?"

"Where abouts do you want me to hit them?"

"Anywhere that'll kill them."

Homer pulled his rifle out of the saddle boot and cranked a shell into the chamber. He raised it to his shoulder and took careful aim. He snapped off a shot, and one of the two cowboys dropped from the saddle. The other cowboy started to ride. Homer chambered another round and aimed again. Taking a little more time because of the moving target, he fired again. The second cowboy dropped to the ground. Homer glanced over at Jules with a smile on his face.

"Good work," said Jules. "Now let's round up them cows."

The murderous gang then turned into a group of working cowhands. It didn't take them long to gather the herd and get it moving. They headed for LeDoux's ranch.

Early the next morning, Charlie Bob rode hard up to the big ranch house. Chaney was standing on the porch with Pearlie, telling her of his plans for the day. When he saw Charlie Bob riding hard, he turned to face the cowboy. Charlie Bob reined in and practically jumped out of the saddle.

"What is it?" said Chaney.

"Someone's took the cattle from the north range," said Charlie Bob. "They killed Jory and Soapy."

"Damn," said Chaney. "Have all the boys gather up here right away. Send someone out for the bodies."

"Right," said Charlie Bob. He turned to remount his horse. Chaney faced Pearlie again.

"It's going to get worse before it gets better," he said.

"I know," she said. "Let's finish it as fast as we can."

"So what the hell is our next move?" Chaney asked.

"I recommend," said Slocum, "that we try to follow the trail of that rustled herd."

"And if we find them?" said Chaney.

"Bring them back," said Pearlie.

"Kill whoever we find with them," Slocum said.

Chaney looked from Slocum to Pearlie with a quizzical expression on his face.

"What else?" she said.

The hands began gathering about then with Charlie Bob, and Slocum went down off the porch to mount his Appaloosa. Chaney put his hands on Pearlie's shoulders and looked her in the eyes. He said something, but Slocum could not hear what he said. In another moment, Chaney stepped to the front of the porch. Slocum figured that just about everyone was gathered up by then.

"I want six men to stay here and guard the ranch," Chaney said. Charlie Bob helped him pick out the six, and the rest, with Chaney, Charlie Bob, and Slocum riding at the head of the bunch, made for the range where the cattle had been. They rode hard all the way out, passing the punchers who had been sent for the bodies. Chaney called to them, telling them to stay at the ranch house to guard it from attack. Chaney's group continued on to the place where the cattle should have been. It did not take long for them to figure out where the incident had taken place, and just a little longer to see what direction the herd had been driven. Wasting no more time, Chaney called out, "Let's go."

They rode hard in the wake of the stolen cattle. They went across open prairie, up into some foothills and down into a low valley. The valley was in open range, and there was no fencing on either side. When they came out on the other end, they were on range owned by LeDoux. Chaney held up a hand to stop the men.

"I could've guessed this," said Chaney.

"What?" Slocum asked.

"LeDoux's range."

"I'd say that makes it pretty damn clear," said Charlie Bob.

"How many men do you see down there?"

"I only make out four," Slocum said, "but I wouldn't count on it."

"What do you mean?"

"There's hills around on two sides," Slocum said. "This could be a trap."

"I don't think so," said Chaney. But he looked around nervously. "Hell, they just stole our cattle is all."

"You reckon they ever doubted who it was you'd suspicion?"

"They know damn well that we know—"

"That's what I'm getting at," said Slocum. "They know that we'd think of them first, and they must be pretty damn sure that we'd come after them. Right?"

"Yeah," Chaney said.

"So what do we do?" said Charlie Bob.

"Slocum?" said Chaney. "This is a little more in your line."

"I'd say let me and three more men ride down there. Give us plenty of time. We'll get down within shooting range of those rannies we can see. If you see anyone pop up his head or show himself in any way, then you come riding in after them."

Chaney and Charlie Bob looked at each other, and Charlie Bob shrugged. Chaney looked at Slocum.

"All right," he said, "but you be careful. Be small comfort if we spy someone hid in the rocks on account of he shoots you."

"We'll be careful," said Slocum. "I ain't itching to get myself shot."

Slocum urged his horse forward, and three cowhands followed him. They made their way slowly down into the next valley. About halfway down, Slocum eased out his Colt. The other riders did the same. They all glanced around themselves all the way down, looking for anyone who might be lurking in the rocks on the hillside. They reached the bottom of the hill without being seen, and then Slocum gave his big

Appaloosa a signal, and it bolted forward. The four riders raced toward the herd and the four rustlers.

Very soon, the rustlers were aware of their approach. One drew a rifle and started to take aim. The others pulled six-guns. "Spread out," said Slocum. "And watch yourselves." None of the rustlers' shots hit their mark. Slocum no longer paid attention to what the other three riders were doing. Now it was every man for himself. He rode up close to the edge of the herd. He snapped off a shot at the man with the rifle and saw him drop from his saddle. Suddenly everyone was shooting. The cattle started bawling and milling around nervously, beginning to cloud the air with dust. Slocum could hear shots all around him. He saw no one fall, but he couldn't be sure. The cattle were moving faster, and the air was filling with dust. It was beginning to be difficult even to hear the shots over the noise of the frightened herd.

Then Slocum saw a form not too far ahead, and it was a man pointing a six-gun at him. Even if it was not one of the rustlers, Slocum did not want to give him a free shot. He raised his Colt and fired quickly. The shape dropped off in the midst of the running cattle, and Slocum heard the man scream. Obviously, his shot had not killed him. It did not matter. The sharp hooves of the cattle would finish the job. Slocum looked around for another target, but the dust was too thick, and he was busy staying out of the way of the insane cattle. He heard another two shots, but he could not tell where they came from.

Up on the side of the hill, Chaney and the others were watching. Chaney was getting nervous, wondering if he should move on in. They had a stampede to take care of. Slocum had told him to wait and watch for any surprise attack, but this business had been going on now for a while and no one had appeared on the hillside. He was about to make a move, when he saw something out of the corner of his eye. He turned his head, and there on the hillside off to his right were six or eight men, mounted and heading down into the fight. His heart pounded in his chest. He drew his six-gun. He waited.

The other men began shooting almost as soon as they had begun to move, but those shots, Chaney knew, were wasted. He let them get about halfway down the hill, and then he called out to his own men, "Let's go." They charged. By the time they got down the hill, the riders were already on the flat valley floor, riding toward Slocum and the others. Chaney and his bunch came up behind them. They were caught. Slocum had been right. Chaney and Charlie Bob and their followers fired into the backs of the LeDoux bunch, dropping them from their horses. The fools did not even suspect what was happening to them.

Slocum was also firing at them from his position in front of the attack. The cattle herd was just about gone in its wild, headlong race, but the air remained thick. It was still hard to see. Soon, however, the shots had stopped. The Snug T boys could find no more targets. In another minute, Chaney rode up beside Slocum.

"Looks like we got them all," he said.

"Looks that way," said Slocum. "We lose anyone?"

"I don't think so, but I ain't sure."

"Why don't you send Charlie Bob and enough hands to stop that stampede and turn the herd back around, so we can drive them home? You and me can stick around here and check all the bodies."

The dust was dying down a bit by then, and Chaney called out to Charlie Bob, giving him the instructions Slocum had suggested. Charlie Bob left two hands with Chaney and Slocum and rode with the rest after the errant cattle. Slocum sat still in his saddle watching the cowboys ride off. Then he rode to the nearest body. He didn't recognize it, but he waited until Chaney rode up beside him to take a look. It was a LeDoux man. Slowly they rode around the battlefield and checked each one. They were all the enemy. Apparently, the Snug T had not lost a man. At last, the other two hands rode up beside Slocum and Chaney.

"What do we do with them?" said one of the men.

"Leave them lay," said Slocum. "They won't know the difference."

"That's all?"

"Unless you want to go through their pockets and see if they have anything you want."

None of the cowboys felt like doing that, so Chaney suggested that they all ride after Charlie Bob and give him a hand. Slocum agreed. It wasn't long before they met the men coming back with the herd. They had the cattle fairly well settled down, although they were still bawling quite a bit. Just about any little thing could have set them off again. Slocum and the other three joined in to do their part. It took the rest of the day to get the herd back on Snug T range. This time they moved them in farther, away from the open range. Chaney left four men with them.

"Watch yourselves," he said. "Don't let no one come sneaking in on you. I'll send some of the boys from the ranch out to relieve you soon as we get back."

When they got close to the ranch house, they could see that something was wrong. They moved a little faster, and then they saw two bodies laid out on the porch. They whipped up their horses and rode the rest of the way in fast. Chaney did a quick dismount and raced up onto the porch. Pearlie came stepping out to meet him and threw her arms around his neck. He hugged her close to him.

"What's happened here?" he said.

"LeDoux's men attacked," Pearlie said. "Our boys fought hard and finally drove them off, but we lost these two here."

She gestured at the two bodies. Chaney looked at them and took the hat off his head.

"Damn," he said.

Slocum came walking up.

"LeDoux's full of surprises," he said. "He split his men. Had the war going on two fronts."

"We still come out ahead," said Chaney.

"Maybe so," Slocum said, "but we can't let him pull that one again."

**8**

"We need to move against him now," Slocum said. "He won't be expecting it."

"Right now?" Chaney said.

"Right now."

Chaney looked over at Pearlie, a question in his eyes.

"Slocum's right, Al," she said. "Finish him off."

"That'd be a bold move," said Chaney.

"That's what's called for," said Slocum. "I say we go over to his ranch and wipe out the whole damn bunch. What's left of them."

"They could be in town. Some of them," Chaney said.

"If we don't get them all at the ranch, then we'll ride on into town," Slocum said, "and take them there. We should've done that the last time."

Chaney bristled under that last comment. He took it as an accusation. He had been the one who counseled against fighting in town, and he knew that Slocum had been itching for a fight. Again he glanced at Pearlie.

"Let's do it," she said.

"How many men?" Chaney asked.

"The whole damn bunch," said Slocum.

"We'd be leaving the ranch unguarded. Pearlie and the ranch."

"I'm going along," Pearlie said. Chaney opened his mouth

to protest, but he saw the determined look on Pearlie's face and decided to keep his trap shut.

"I don't think anyone'll be coming this way," said Slocum. "Not just yet. If we catch them all, either at their ranch or in town, they won't be coming this way ever again."

"All right, hell," said Chaney, "let's mount up and ride."

The attack came as a total surprise to the LeDoux bunch. When the Snug T crowd came barreling onto the ranch, there were two gunslingers lounging on the porch. As soon as they realized what was happening, they jumped up, pulling their irons out. One of them shouted a warning. The other one ran into the house. Someone from the Snug T fired a shot that dropped the one there on the porch. The Snug T hands soon had the LeDoux ranch house surrounded, and they were pouring bullets into the walls and the windows. The men inside began returning fire and dropped a couple of Snug T hands. Slocum dismounted and found some cover there in the yard, and almost immediately, the rest of the Snug T hands did the same.

Pressed behind the trunk of a large tree in the middle of the yard, Slocum suddenly felt a shot come close to his head from another direction. He looked and realized that there were some hands over in the corral and bunkhouse shooting from there. He readjusted himself behind the tree and snapped off a shot in that direction. A man at the corral dropped dead.

"Look toward the bunkhouse," he shouted.

Soon the war was raging on two fronts. The Snug T bunch hit all the men in the corral, but it was tougher to get at those who were inside. Slocum realized that something else had to be done. He checked his pocket for matches. Then he ducked low and ran for the house. A man at a window saw him and raised a rifle. From her position behind some bales of hay, Pearlie raised her own rifle and snapped off a shot. The man dropped his weapon and fell, laying out through the window. Slocum made it safely to the side of the ranch house. Squatting down, he pressed himself against the wall and looked around. Quickly, he scooped up a pile of dried grass and twigs, anything he could reach that would burn, and struck a match to it. Taking off his hat, he fanned the blaze. Soon it was crawling up the side of the ranch house. He stood up and ran to the back corner of the house and waited, six-gun in hand, watching the back door.

Shots were still sounding rapidly all around. Even so, in another minute he could hear loud voices coming from inside the house. Someone yelled, "They've set fire to the house! They're trying to burn us out!" Another one shouted, "I'd rather get shot than burned alive!" Slocum waited. It was another couple of minutes before the first of the LeDoux gunmen came running out the back door. Slocum dropped him in his tracks. Another one followed, and someone else, one of the Snug T men behind the house, shot that one. Others must have been pouring out the front door. It wasn't long before the shots came more slowly. No one else came out the back door.

Slocum moved carefully to the front of the house. Chaney and Pearlie and other Snug T hands were standing in the yard, emerging from their cover. The shooting had almost stopped. Then another shot rang out from the bunkhouse, and one of the Snug T boys fell dead there in the yard. The rest quickly ducked back under cover. "There's still some in the bunkhouse," Chaney yelled.

Slocum led the way, running for the cover of a tree that stood closer to the bunkhouse. Others followed his lead, closing in. Once again, the shots were fast and furious, shattering all the bunkhouse windows and ripping through the thin plank walls. Slocum ducked low and ran again, making it this time all the way to the corral. A face appeared at a window and a gun hand poked out. Slocum fired quickly, and the face fell away from the window. Still keeping low, Slocum ran for the door. When he reached it, he bashed it open with his shoulder and threw himself inside. He saw three gunmen in there, and he fired quickly, dropping all three. The fight was over.

He walked back outside and called out, "They're all dead over here."

The rest of his outfit emerged from cover once again. They all gathered together in the yard in front of the blazing ranch house. They stood looking around at the bodies in the yard. A couple of them were their own boys. Pearlie looked at the flaming ranch house. "There's no one left in there," she said.

"Let's check the bodies and see who we got," said Chaney. A couple of men walked around behind the house. Slocum, Chaney, Pearlie and the others checked out the bodies in the front yard. "Does anyone know how many hands LeDoux had?" Slocum asked.

"It looks to me like we got damn near all of them," Chaney said.

A man came walking back from behind the blaze. "LeDoux's back there, dead," he said.

"Well, that should do it," said Pearlie.

"I don't see that Jules around anywhere," said Flank Steak.

"You're right," said Charlie Bob. "He wasn't one of them out back neither."

"Check those in the bunkhouse," Slocum said.

Just then the sound of pounding hooves caused them all to look toward the corral. A man hunkered low over the neck of his mount was heading hard out toward the far side of the ranch. Chaney pulled out his six-gun and fired two rapid shots at the man, but they were both wide.

"Damn," he said.

"That's one that got away," said Flank Steak.

They walked out to the bunkhouse to check the bodies there, but Jules was not one of them. They decided that he was likely the one that rode away fast. They couldn't worry about him just then. With LeDoux dead, there was no one left to pay Jules anyway. He would probably just ride on, get the hell out of the territory. If he did not run away, he would most likely go into town. The only thing left to worry about was Comstock, but even he was on LeDoux's payroll. He would likely skedaddle along with Jules, if Jules had ridden to town to warn him. But Slocum wanted to get them anyway. He did not want anyone getting away. He recalled the way that Comstock and his "posse" had murdered poor Tyson.

"Let's head for town," he said.

Jules had damn near ruined the horse he had ridden into Hangout, and when he got there, he just jumped out of the saddle and abandoned the poor animal in the street. He ran into the sheriff's office but found it empty. He ran out and across the street to the Bird's Beak Saloon. Inside, he found Comstock sitting at a table nursing a bottle of whiskey. He hurried over to the table, gasping for breath.

"Comstock," he said, panting.

Comstock looked up. "Jules," he said, "what the hell's wrong with you? Sit down and have a drink. Catch your breath."

"There ain't time," Jules said, still breathing heavily. "That Snug T outfit . . . They just wiped us out . . . out at the ranch . . ."

"What?"

"LeDoux's dead. Everyone but me."

"God damn," said Comstock, standing up so quickly that he knocked over his chair. "Are you sure about that?"

"Everyone's dead. It's just you and me."

"Come on," said Comstock. He led the way out of the Bird's Beak and over to the sheriff's office, where he opened the safe and took out the money that was in there. It wasn't a lot, but it was all he could put his hands on quickly. Then he hurried down the street to the stable with Jules right behind him. Both men saddled up and rode out of the stable and quickly out of town, in the opposite direction from LeDoux's ranch.

When Slocum and the Snug T outfit rode into Hangout, some people ducked inside buildings. Others just stood on the street eyeing them with curiosity. They had all the look of a gang of banditti on the prowl, and that's just about what they were. They stopped at the sheriff's office and found it empty.

They rode on over to the Bird's Beak. They dismounted, all of them, and went inside. At the bar, Slocum said to the barkeep, "We're looking for Comstock and Jules." The barkeep thought about playing dumb, his usual attitude when questioned, but he looked at the large gang of Snug T men, and the one woman with them, and changed his mind.

"Comstock was in here earlier," he said, "but Jules come running in and told him something, and the two of the hurried on out of here real fast."

Pearlie turned her back to the barkeep and faced the crowd in the saloon. "Did anyone in here see what direction they went?" she asked in a loud voice.

"Comstock and Jules," said Chaney. "Did anyone see them leave here?"

A man sitting at a table near the door said, "They looked to me like they was headed for the sheriff's office."

"Anyone else see anything?" said Slocum.

There was a pause, and then another man spoke up. "I was just coming in here," he said. "I seen them go into the stable."

"Did you see them come out again?" Pearlie asked.

"I wasn't paying no attention," the man said. "Hell, I come on in here. I didn't know nothing was going on."

"Let's go," said Slocum. They walked down to the stable. The stable man was mucking stalls. He stopped, hesitant, when he saw the big crowd.

"What's going on here?" he asked.

Chaney stepped up close to the man. "I'll ask the questions," he said. "Comstock and Jules was seen coming in here. Where'd they go from here?"

"I don't know," the man said. "I just got back from my lunch. I never seen them." He stood looking around. "There's two horses missing though. Saddles, too. One of them belongs to Comstock. Looks to me like the other one's been stole."

Slocum, Chaney and the rest walked back to the sheriff's office.

"The safe's standing open," Chaney said.

"It looks like he cleaned it out in a hurry," said Pearlie.

"Likely they headed out of town in that direction," said Slocum, pointing. "I don't think they'd ride toward where they knew we was at."

"We going after them?" asked Flank Steak.

Chaney looked toward Pearlie and then Slocum.

"Not all of us," Slocum said. "Hell, there's just the two of them."

"I'll go," said Chaney, "and—"

"No," said Slocum. "You got a ranch to run, and now you won't have no one interfering with you. I'll go."

"At least take a couple of boys with you," Pearlie said.

"When I can't handle two like that by my own self," Slocum said, "I'll hang up my guns."

"I'll feel better," said Pearlie. "Take them along, for me."

Slocum looked over the crowd of Snug T hands. "Charlie Bob," he said, "you want to go along?"

"You damn rights," said Charlie Bob.

"I'll go, too," said Flank Steak.

Slocum looked back at Pearlie. "That all right with you?" he asked.

"Of course," she said. "Let's get you outfitted for the trail."

Pearlie walked over to a small café, where she ordered up the kind of food that was good for the trail. While they waited, Slocum and the men—all except Chaney, who stayed with Pearlie—went into the Bird's Beak for a drink of whiskey. They finished one and ordered another. Chaney came walking in. He stopped at the bar beside Slocum. "We've got you ready to go," he said. "We picked up some extra ammunition, too."

"Good," said Slocum. He downed the rest of his drink and turned to the two cowboys who were riding with him. "You boys ready?" he said.

"You bet," said Charlie Bob.

"Any time you say," said Flank Steak.

They all walked out into the street, where Pearlie gave them the goods she had just purchased. Slocum and the two cowboys stuffed the food and ammunition into their saddle-bags and mounted up. They were about to head out of town when Chaney stopped them.

"Slocum," he said, "the faster you catch up with them the better."

"How come?" Slocum asked.

"Well, I don't know what Comstock's thinking, but the direction he's headed, he could be on his way to the capital."

Slocum gave Chaney an inquisitive look.

"If he shows up there and tells some big lies, we could all be in real trouble."

"I don't believe the governor would believe anything against us," said Pearlie. "He and my uncle were good friends, but he does know Comstock as the sheriff, and you never know."

"Catch them, Slocum," said Chaney.

"And be careful," Pearlie added.

## 9

Slocum, Charlie Bob and Flank Steak took off on the trail of Comstock and Jules. It was a simple trail to follow at first, but a few miles out of town, it disappeared. They stopped riding, dismounted and looked around. The tracks had simply vanished.

"What the hell?" said Flank Steak.

"Maybe they took off a-flying," said Charlie Bob.

"It looks that way," said Slocum. He stepped up again into the saddle, turning his Appaloosa back toward town.

Flank Steak remounted, too. "What you fixing to do, Slocum?" he asked.

"Backtrack," Slocum said.

Charlie Bob was in the saddle again as well, and the three men rode slowly back over their own trail. After about a mile, Slocum spotted a small trail heading off to the left and rising up into the mountains there. He studied it for a while. "It looks like they might've turned off here," he said.

"We'd a been paying more attention, we might've saw it a while ago," said Flank Steak.

"Well, the tracks aren't all that clear," Slocum said. "The trail's rocky, but it looks like someone rode up there not too long ago. Since Comstock and that other feller seem to have vanished on us, it could be they rode up this way. Where's it go?"

"It just crosses the mountains here is all," said Charlie Bob. "It don't really go nowhere."

"They sure ain't headed for the capital," said Flank Steak. "Not going that away."

"Maybe they've give it up," said Charlie Bob. "Maybe they's just trying to get away with what they got."

"Maybe," Slocum said. "Come on."

He urged his mount onto the trail and started riding up. Charlie Bob followed and Flank Steak moved in close behind.

"Could be they're just trying to throw us off," said Charlie Bob. "Could be when they get across the mountains, they'll turn north again. Then when they get far enough up there, they'll recross the mountains and come on down in the capital. It's sure enough the long way, but it could be that's what they're up to."

"Could be," Slocum said. "It damn near worked."

"What are we going to do when we catch them, Slocum?" Flank Steak said.

"Kill them."

"Just like that?"

"That's what they did to Mr. Tyson," Slocum said. "They don't deserve any better."

Up toward the top of the mountain, Comstock was leading the way. Jules was coming along not far behind. Comstock rode up beside a large boulder nestled in a clump of smaller ones. He stopped his horse and studied the site for a moment, then looked back down the trail. Jules came alongside him. Comstock pointed back down the trail.

"You got a clear view here for a good ways down," he said.

Jules looked back and agreed.

"If anyone's following us," Comstock said, "they likely missed us when we turned off the main road."

"That's what I figure," said Jules.

"Just in case they didn't, though," Comstock said, "I want you to get back behind that big rock and watch the trail."

"What are you going to do?"

"I'm going on to the capital. The sooner I get there the better. I'll tell the governor my version of what went on back there in Hangout. I'll get some more deputies, and then we'll go back and get those bastards."

"I thought we was just clearing out with the money," Jules said.

"We got a big stake in Hangout," Comstock said. "It's a gold mine. I don't aim to turn loose of it."

"LeDoux had all that stuff," Jules said. "He's dead. How can we make any profit off of that?"

"You ever hear tell of a sheriff's auction?"

"Yeah."

"Well, hell, we'll have one; only no one'll know about it except just you and me."

"Yeah?"

"Yeah. And this time, it'll be you and me. No one in the way like before. We'll make us a lot more money than what LeDoux ever paid us. Now get around behind that rock and watch."

"Comstock?"

"What?"

"How long do I watch before I decide they ain't coming?"

"A couple of hours ought to do it. I'll be in the capital. Find me there."

"Hey. What if they are coming?"

"Kill them. You got a good line of fire here. They'll be coming uphill. You'll do all right."

Comstock rode on ahead, leaving Jules to take care of things there on the uphill trail. For a moment, Jules watched Comstock ride. Then he took his own horse back around the far side of the big boulder. He dismounted and tied the horse. Then he took the rifle out of the scabbard and moved over to the rock. He checked around, found the most likely spot and settled in. Looking down the trail, he thought about Comstock. The sheriff had all of the money. What if he just rode on with it? What if he abandoned Jules to fight it out here on the trail while he rode off miles away, not leaving any word anywhere about the direction of his travels? Jules wondered if he was being played for a fool. He thought about mounting up again and chasing after Comstock, demanding that they split the cash right there. Or maybe even shooting the sheriff in the back and taking all of the money for himself.

He did not move though. He stayed snugged down there by the boulder and kept his eyes peeled on the trail below. He wondered how he would know when a couple of hours had gone by. Time seemed to be dragging. He had no idea how long he had been watching. It couldn't have been but a few minutes, yet it seemed much longer. Hell, he thought, there's no one down there. He took out the makings and rolled himself a cigarette. Taking a match out of his pocket, he scratched it on the side of the boulder and lit his smoke. He kept watching, but there was no one down there. He smoked the rest of his cigarette, then snubbed it out in the dirt between his feet. There was still no sign of anyone on the trail.

Comstock had ridden to the top of the mountain and was on his way down the other side. He was moving along at a steady pace. When he got to the capital, he would seek an audience with the governor. If the governor was busy or otherwise not available, he would tell them that it was emergency. He was the sheriff over at Hangout. They would have to listen to him. He did not anticipate any trouble getting in to see the governor. Then he would tell the governor that Slocum, a professional gunman, had come into Hangout and murdered several people, including Tyson, LeDoux and all of his own deputies except Jules. He needed a warrant for Slocum, and he needed authorization to hire additional men.

He knew better than to accuse Tyson or any of the Snug T people, because it was well known that Tyson and the governor had been good friends. He would have to be careful how he played his cards, and it was crucial that he get to the governor before anyone from the Snug T. He did not think that the Snug T outfit would be in any hurry to get to the capital, for they had just won the war, or so it seemed. Hell, he thought, they probably figured that he and Jules had skipped the country. He thought about Jules.

Jules was a pretty good man in a pinch, and it would be well if Jules survived whatever might happen back there on the trail. But if he didn't, that would be all right, too. If anyone was on their trail, and if Jules saw them coming and there was a fight back there, that would slow down their pursuit and give Comstock that much more time. If Jules should have to die, well, hell, he would die for a good cause. Comstock felt pretty smug. After all, he was the sheriff.

"Al," said Pearlie, "do you think Slocum and the boys will be all right?"

"Slocum can sure handle himself," Chaney said. "And those two boys are no slouches. I wouldn't worry bout them, Pearlie."

They were sitting together side by side on the front porch of the big ranch house.

"Do you think we should post some guards around the ranch tonight?"

"We've won the fight with LeDoux. Comstock has run off. I'd say we're pretty safe right now. Safer than we've been for a long time."

"I'd still feel better."

"All right," said Chaney. "If it'll make you feel better, I'll put a few of the boys around on watch for the night."

"Thanks, Al." She paused for a few seconds, then added, "I'll just feel a whole lot better when Slocum gets back and tells us that he's got Comstock."

"Yeah," said Chaney. "I think we all will."

Slocum stopped his Appaloosa and looked ahead. A ways up above was a cluster of small boulders with a large one protruded from its center. It looked to Slocum like anyone behind the big boulder would have a clear view of a considerable portion of the trail down below.

"What is it, Slocum?" said Charlie Bob.

"This is a pretty good spot for an ambush," Slocum said.

"We don't even know there's anyone up there," said Charlie Bob.

"You want to find out when someone takes a shot at you?" said Slocum.

"That ain't my favorite way," Charlie Bob admitted.

"Say," said Flank Steak, "I'm a pretty fair mountain goat. I reckon I could leave the trail and make my way around behind them rocks and take a look."

Slocum looked around at the surrounding terrain. "You pretty sure you could do that?"

"Take me a little while," Flank Steak said, "but I can damn sure do it."

"All right then," Slocum said. "Have at it."

Flank Steak dismounted and tied his horse. Then he slipped off the trail and into the rocks off to his own left. In a matter of seconds, he had disappeared from the sight of Slocum and Charlie Bob. The two sat still and listened. They could hear nothing. Flank Steak was mighty quiet out there. Slocum slipped out his Winchester and cranked a shell into the chamber. The noise seemed particularly loud in the silence.

Flank Steak moved quietly over and between the rocks, moving in a straight line to his left. In a few moments, though, he changed direction and started straight up. If he calculated right, he would come out behind the clump of boulder they had spotted. He reached to take hold of a rock, but it was loose. He let go and found another. Testing it, he found it solid, and he pulled himself up with it, searching carefully for footholds as he did. Now and then, the ground would level off some, and he would have an easy few steps. Then it would get steep again, and he would have to slow down and pick his way cautiously over the rocks, sometimes round, sometimes jagged. He gauged that he was about halfway through his climb when he came to a level spot, and he stopped to catch his breath.

Up above, Jules was bored as hell. As yet, he had seen nothing. He was getting suspicious of Comstock again. Again he was thinking of abandoning his post and getting after the sheriff to protect his own interests. He did not though. Instead, he took out his makings again and rolled another cigarette. As he lit it, he wondered just how long he had been sitting there, how much longer he would stay.

Down on the trail, Slocum saw a plume of smoke rise up from behind the big boulder. He looked back at Charlie Bob and nodded his head. Charlie Bob saw the smoke and pulled out his own rifle, chambering a shot. Neither man spoke. They watched the clump of boulders carefully.

Flank Steak figured that he was about even with the boulders, and so he started working his way back to his right. He moved slowly. Soon he saw the large boulder. He kept going. There was another clump of rocks between Flank Steak and the big boulder he was aiming for. He made his way around it, and then he saw the man. He was sitting beside the large boulder, his rifle propped against it, and he was smoking. Flank Steak was almost directly behind the man. He was not in a position for a good shot, however, because his footing was awkward. He eased the revolver out of his holster and moved slowly a few more steps toward the man. At last, he felt secure in his footing. He was close enough for a good shot with the revolver, too. He held it up and aimed it at the man's back. Then he cocked it.

The sound alerted Jules, who reached for his rifle and turned at the same time. Flank Steak yelled, "Hold it," but just then his foot slipped, and he landed hard on his butt. Jules was standing. He raised the rifle to his shoulder and aimed at the now helpless Flank Steak. Down below, Slocum could see Jules when he stood. He raised his Winchester and fired a quick shot. It spanged against the boulder just over Jules's shoulder. Jules turned again and dropped back out of sight. Flank Steak scrambled to his feet and found some cover. "Damn," he said.

"That you up there, Jules?" Slocum called out.

"It's me."

"Throw out your guns and come on out."

"Fuck you. Come and get me."

"There's three of us, Jules, and one is up there behind you."

"I said come and get me," Jules yelled, and he popped up just long enough to fire a shot down the trail. Then he disappeared again. The shot whizzed past Slocum just on his right and knocked the hat off of Charlie Bob's head.

"God damn," said Charlie Bob.

"Hey, Jules," said Slocum. "Where's Comstock? He leave you behind to slow us down? You're just buying him time, Jules, and you're fixing to pay for it with your life."

Jules began to panic. He knew about Slocum. He was a dangerous man, and he had said that he had another one down there with him. Then there was the third one behind him. Jules wondered where that one had gone. He looked back in that direction, but he could no longer see the man. He could be anywhere out there. Comstock had surely played him for a fool. Slocum was right about that. But it was too late to do anything about it. He knew that Slocum wanted him dead. He had been along with Comstock when they had killed Tyson, and Slocum would recognize him almost for sure. He would just have to fight it out and hope for the best. He pressed himself against the big boulder and began inching himself around to the top side. He had moved only a little ways when he spotted Flank Steak.

He raised his rifle once again, but Flank Steak saw him as well, and Flank Steak popped off a shot from his revolver. The bullet struck Jules in the left shoulder. He yelped and stood up, giving Slocum a near perfect target. Slocum fired, and Jules fell over on the rocks. He rolled over on his back to die, and his body slid about ten feet down the side of the mountain in the loose rocks.

# 10

It was dark, and the sentries had been sent out. Chaney was back on the porch with Pearlie. They were sitting in the same chairs as before, side by side. They had been silent for a space, and then Chaney spoke up again.

"I keep thinking about Slocum and those two boys," he said. "I sure hope they make out all right."

"You said it yourself, Al," said Pearlie. "Slocum can handle himself, and Charlie Bob and Flank Steak are no slouches either. Try to relax. It's been a long, hard fight. Now it's about over. The LeDoux bunch is gone. There's no one left from the other side but Comstock. He shouldn't be any problem. We can get things back to normal here."

"Yeah," said Chaney, but he still had a bit of worry in his voice.

Pearlie suddenly stood up. "Come on, Al," she said.

"Where?"

"Come in the house with me. I think you could use a good stiff drink."

Chaney stood up. "I won't argue with that," he said. He followed Pearlie into the house. She latched the door and gestured toward the big overstuffed couch, and he walked over to it and sat down. Pearlie moved over to a large cabinet that stood against a far wall. She took down two glasses which she then poured half full with good whiskey. She

76

picked up the glasses and walked over to the couch. She handed one glass to Chaney and sat down beside him. Lifting her own glass, she said, "Here's to peace and quiet and good hard ranch work."

"I'll drink tô that," Chaney said, and they each took a tentative sip.

"Al," she said, "I don't know what I'd do without you."

"I hope you don't ever find out," he said. He took another sip, and so did she.

Comstock rode into the capital city after dark, and went straight to the governor's mansion. Tying his horse to the hitch post, he walked boldly up on the porch. He was met by an armed guard at the front door.

"Hold it, mister," the guard said. "Where do you think you're going?"

"I need to see the governor," Comstock said.

"He'll be in his office in the morning at nine o'clock," said the guard.

"I'm Sheriff Comstock from over at Hangout, and this is an emergency. If it wasn't, I wouldn't be here this time of night. I've got to see him now."

"It'll wait till morning."

"I don't believe it will," Comstock said. "There's a professional killer on my trail right now. I could be dead by morning."

The guard looked suspiciously at Comstock.

"Hell, man, tell the governor that his old friend Reggie Tyson has already been murdered."

The guard turned and rapped on the door.

Slocum set a leisurely pace, and the two cowhands rode one on either side of him. As they moved along, Charlie Bob said, "Slocum, don't you think we'd oughta ride a little faster? Comstock'll be getting into the capital before long. We need to get there before he does."

"We don't need to kill our horses doing it," Slocum said.

"Even if he gets there before us," Flank Steak said, "he

won't be able to do no business till morning, will he?"

"That's what I'm counting on," said Slocum.

"What can the son of a bitch do anyhow?" Flank Steak said.

"He can make up some lies to tell on us," said Charlie Bob.

"The governor ain't likely to believe no lies told on Mr. Tyson nor any of the Snug T outfit," Flank Steak said. "Hell, Mr. Tyson and him was pals a long time back."

"I'm counting on that, too," Slocum said. "Come on. We can pick up the pace now for a little while."

Pearlie and Al Chaney were stripped naked. They were still sitting on the couch together, and they were wrapped in each other's arms. Chaney had a hand on one of Pearlie's ample breasts and was gently kneading it. Their lips were pressed together, and Pearlie moaned low in her throat. She let a hand drift down between Chaney's legs, and she found his balls, heavy in their sack. She slipped her hand underneath them and hefted them. Then she squeezed them gently. Chaney groaned, and Pearlie slid her hand upward to find his stiff rod standing up straight and hard against his belly. She gripped it, and it bucked and throbbed in her clutch.

"Oooh, Al," she said.

"Oh, God, Pearlie," said Chaney.

Comstock was led into a waiting room in the governor's mansion, and the governor was standing there in a smoking jacket with a drink in his hand. His expression was stern. Before the crooked sheriff could open his mouth, the governor said, "What's this about Reggie Tyson?"

"I'm sorry to be the one to have to tell you, Governor," said Comstock, "but he's dead."

"How?"

"Murdered. Ambushed on the trail."

"Reggie never even carried a gun."

"That's right, Sir. It was deliberate and cold-blooded."

"Have you apprehended the murderer?"

"No, sir. That's—"

"Then what the hell are you doing here?"

Comstock's mind raced. He knew that he could say nothing bad about Tyson or any of his people. He would have to be damned careful what he said.

"We had a range war develop over there near Hangout," he said. "It was going on almost before I knowed anything about it. I was trying to sort things out, you know, talking to both parties, when—"

"What two parties?"

"Mr. Tyson and LeDoux."

"I knew that damned LeDoux would be trouble," said the governor.

"Well, sir, yes. You were right about that." Comstock's mind was racing. "He went and hired a professional killer. A man named Slocum."

"Slocum," said the governor. "Slocum. I seem to have heard that name."

"He's a notorious son of a bitch, sir. Oh, excuse me. I beg your pardon. But he is a notorious gunfighter. He has a bad reputation. A real mean one. Well, whenever, uh, Le-Doux hired him, he went and ambushed poor Mr. Tyson. Killed him real brutal."

"Damn it," said the governor.

"He's killed all my deputies, too."

"What can I do?"

"I need authorization to hire on a band of new deputies. LeDoux is wiped out, but Slocum's still running wild through my territory. He ain't going to be easy to run down."

"How many men do you think you need?"

"I could probably manage with about six or eight."

"I'll authorize eight," said the governor. "Do you know where you can find the men? I can help with that if you need it."

"Oh, no, sir. Thank you, but I'm sure I can find the men I need."

"And, Sheriff, you be sure and keep me informed. I want to know when you catch this goddamned Slocum."

"You'll be the first to know, Governor. I promise you that."

Pearlie had laid back on the big couch, spreading her legs and pulling Chaney after her. He was on top of her, between her legs, his rampant rod thrusting in and out of her soft and delicate pussy. Pearlie thrust her hips up against him as he drove into her. They were raging like wild beasts.

"Oh, fuck me, Al," she said. "Fuck me."

"Ah, God," he said, as he felt the pressure build up in his loins. He pounded harder and faster, and suddenly he burst forth into her depths, gush after gush. Spent at last, he lay still, gasping for breath. Pearlie continued humping against him, till at last he slipped out. He straightened up and sat back against the couch, still panting. Pearlie moved in front of him.

"Can you go again?" she asked.

"Oh," said Chaney. "I don't know."

"Let's find out," she said, and she knelt in front of him on the floor between his knees. She lifted his wilting willy, feeling the sticky substance that coated it, that was her own juices, and she slurped it into her mouth, sucking it clean. As she did, Chaney moaned and groaned with painful pleasure, and the rod stiffened again, rising up anxiously. Pearlie bounced her head up and down a few more times. Then she got up abruptly, crawled back onto the couch on her hands and knees and said, "Get behind me."

Comstock swaggered into the Palace Saloon armed with his authorization from the governor. He walked straight to the bar and ordered a shot of whiskey, which he downed in one gulp. Then he ordered another. Taking it in his left hand, he turned his back to the bar and leaned on his elbows. He surveyed the crowd. He saw some that appeared to be local businessmen, a few cowhands, one or two he took to be drummers. Back in the far corner, he noticed five tough-looking hombres sitting together at a table. He squinted, trying to recognize them. At last he thought that he knew one of the men. It was a man he had run out of Hangout a few years earlier. A no-good gunfighter called Slab. He turned back to the barkeep and paid for the bottle. Then he took it and his glass and headed for Slab's table. As he came near, he could see Slab tense up. His four companions followed his lead. They were all braced for trouble. Comstock stopped close to the table.

"Hello, Slab," he said.

"What the hell do you want?"

"A little talk is all. Can I buy you boys a drink?" Comstock held out the bottle.

"You're out of your county, Comstock," Slab said. "Besides that, I ain't wanted for nothing in these parts."

"Neither are any of the rest of us," said the man seated to Slab's right.

"I ain't looking for trouble with you boys," Comstock said. "Like I done told you, I want to talk and buy you a drink."

Slab looked around the table at his companions and finally shrugged. "Sit down," he said.

There was one chair unoccupied at the table, and Comstock put down his bottle and glass and pulled out the chair to sit down. He poured himself a drink and pushed the bottle over to Slab. Slab poured one and started the bottle around the table. When everyone had a drink, Comstock spoke up again.

"You want to introduce your friends?" he said.

"Boys," said Slab, "this here is Sheriff Comstock from over at Hangout. He run me out of his town a couple of years back."

"Water under the bridge," Comstock said.

Nodding at the man on his right, Slab said, "This is Riley Hill." Then going on around the table he continued. "Chester Barker, Tod McCool, Art Bacon."

"Nice meeting you fellows," Comstock said.

"Why don't you cut out the bullshit," said Bacon, "and tell us what the hell you're after?"

Comstock lifted his glass for another sip. "You boys working?" he asked.

"You might say we're in between jobs," Slab said.

"You looking for work?"

"Could be. Depends on what it is."

"I'm looking for eight new deputies."

Slab laughed. "Deputies?" he said. "You got to be funning us." He reached for the bottle to refill his glass. "But go on. I like a good joke."

The bottle got passed around the table again and made its way back to Comstock. He refilled his own glass, lifted it and took a sip.

"It's no joke, Slab," he said. "I need eight good men who ain't afraid of a fight. I got me a gunfighter over to Hangout I need to get rid of."

"One gunfighter?" said McCool.

"He's tough enough," Comstock said.

"I reckon," said Slab, "if you're looking for eight men to go after just one."

"We might have to split up and hunt for him," said the sheriff. "And whenever we do find him, it'll damn sure take more than one man to face him."

"Do you want this man caught or killed?" said McCool.

"I don't want to see him alive again," Comstock said. "Not if I can help it."

"What are you paying?" Slab asked.

"Better'n regular deputy pay," said Comstock. "Plus, I'll pay the man who gets Slocum a thousand dollars."

"Slocum?" said Hill.

"That's what he calls himself."

"I've heard of this Slocum," Hill said. "He's a dangerous son of a bitch. I hear tell he can take on three men at once all by his lonesome."

"You scared?" Comstock said.

No one answered Comstock's question. Instead, Slab asked one of his own. "Suppose we get rid of this Slocum for you," he said. "Is the job over?"

"It could be," said Comstock, "and you'd have money in

your jeans, but likely it won't be. There's a couple of ranches over near Hangout that I want to take over. One of them'll be pretty easy to get. The other one could be a little more trouble. Get rid of Slocum, and take over them two ranches for me, that's just the beginning. I'm already the sheriff. Them deputy jobs could turn out to be permanent. We could be running the whole damn territory."

Slab finished his drink and looked each of his partners in the face. "Let's give it a try, boys," he said. "What do you say?"

They all agreed, and another round was poured. Comstock drank his with a great deal of relish. He put down his glass and asked, "You boys got rooms here?"

"We got a camp just outside of town," Slab said.

"All right," said Comstock. "We'll get up and have us a breakfast in the morning, and then we'll head right on over to Hangout."

It was late when Slocum and the two Snug T cowhands rode into the capital, but there were still people moving about on the sidewalks and still plenty of horses tied at the hitch rails in front of saloons and eating joints. Slocum stopped riding just inside the city.

"Whatcha doing?" said Charlie Bob.

Slocum looked down the street. "There's no telling where that son of a bitch might be," he said.

"If he's even here," said Flank Steak.

"Yeah," said Slocum. "Tell you what. Let's split up and search the whole damn town. If he's here, and he's still up and about, we'll find him."

# 11

Slocum rode down to the far end of Main Street, leaving
Flank Steak and Charlie Bob to work the other end of town.
He started by looking in the first saloon he came to. He saw
no one he recognized. He came to an eating establishment
next and checked that out with the same results. Soon he had
been in three saloons and four eating joints, including one
fairly nice restaurant, and there had been no sign of Comstock. He saw a fine-looking house which someone identified
for him as the governor's mansion, but he saw no sign of
Comstock's horse there. In fact, there was no horse at all tied
to the hitch posts in front of the mansion. He went back to
checking saloons and eating places. He went into one hotel
and checked the register. No Comstock.

At the other end of Main Street, Charlie Bob had taken
one side of the street and Flank Steak the other. They were
using the same method as Slocum, checking saloons, eating
places and hotels. Charlie Bob walked into a place called the
Palace Saloon. He looked around and was about to turn
around and leave again when he took a second look at a
table with six men sitting there. One of the men with his
back to Charlie Bob had a familiar look to him. Charlie Bob
walked in farther and took a place at the bar. He ordered a
shot of whiskey and glanced around casually, taking a better
look at the man. Sure enough, it was Comstock. Charlie Bob

did not think that Comstock knew him or would recognize him, but he couldn't be absolutely sure of that. Still, he had to find out a little bit more about what was going on. He eased himself on down the bar slowly until he was close enough to eavesdrop.

"It's getting late, boys," he heard Comstock say. "If we're going to get an early start, we ought to turn in."

"You're right, Boss," said one of the men. "Let's just have one more round and finish off this bottle."

"Okay," said Comstock. "I'll ride out to your camp with you and spend the night there. Then we can get an early start in the morning."

Charlie Bob finished his drink and went outside. He looked across the street just in time to see Flank Steak coming out of a hotel over there. He gave a shrill whistle, and Flank Steak looked around and saw him. Charlie Bob waved an arm, and Flank Steak hustled on over to meet him.

"What's up?" Flank Steak said.

"He's right in there," said Charlie Bob, "and he's got hisself five new men. You get on down the street and find Slocum. I'll stay here and keep an eye on the bastards."

Flank Steak went back to where he had left his horse and mounted up, then turned and headed down the street as fast as he dared with all the traffic that was still bustling there in the capital. Charlie Bob found a chair there on the street, sat down and rolled himself a cigarette. It took Flank Steak a few minutes to locate Slocum and tell him what Charlie Bob had found. Slocum rode back down the street with Flank Steak. They tied their horses across the street from where Charlie Bob was sitting. Then Slocum remembered that Comstock had an eye for his horse.

"I'm going to take my horse around behind the building here," he said to Flank Steak. "I'll be right back."

He took the big Appaloosa around to the back of the building and tied him there. Then he walked back around to the front and rejoined Flank Steak. He made a motion to Charlie Bob. Charlie Bob stood up, took a final drag on his cigarette, tossed it away and walked across the street, dodging horses and wagons. He walked up to Slocum and Flank Steak.

"He's right inside that place across the street," he said. "He's got five men with him, and I heared one of them call him boss. He said something about laying over at their camp outside of town and then getting an early start in the morning."

"What did the men look like?" said Slocum.

"They all looked like tough customers to me," said Charlie Bob.

"There's five of them?" said Flank Steak.

"Six counting Comstock," said Charlie Bob.

"We could take them," said Flank Steak.

"Not here on the main street of the capital," said Slocum. "Maybe not at all. We don't know who these men are."

He really did think that they might have a fair chance. After all, it would only be two to one, but he did not like to think about taking a chance with the lives of the two cowhands. Of course they had been fighting before, but somehow that seemed different. Slocum did not like the odds. Not this time. Not with the lives of these two boys.

"Let's just stay here and watch them," he said. "See what they do."

They found chairs on the sidewalk, sat down, propped their feet up on the hitch rail and watched the saloon across the street. Slocum took out a cigar and lit it. In just a few minutes, Comstock and his new deputies came out. Slocum recognized Slab and Tod McCool. He knew them as professional gunmen. The other three had the same look about them, but they were strangers to Slocum. As the six men mounted their horses, Slocum noticed Flank Steak and Charlie Bob stiffen.

"Take it easy," he said. "Just let them ride on out."

He continued to puff on his cigar as the six men rode out of town. Finally, when they were out of sight, Slocum stood up. Charlie Bob and Flank Steak stood up with him. They looked at him.

"Get your horses," he said. "I'll be right with you."

He walked around behind the building to retrieve his Appaloosa. When he came riding back, he found the two cowhands waiting for him, mounted and ready to ride. They rode out of town after Comstock and the five deputies.

"We going to take them out on the trail?" Flank Steak said.

"Nope."

"At their campsite?"

"Nope."

"Well, what are we going to do?" said Charlie Bob.

"We ain't going to take on six of them at one time," Slocum said. "I want you boys to go on back to the Snug T and tell them there what's happened. I'll be around, and I'll be watching those six. I want you to just forget about them. Leave it up to me."

"Hell, Slocum," said Flank Steak, "we can't do that. There's six of them, and you—"

"I'll be wanting to know what they're up to. You boys can find out more by staying at the ranch. You can ride into town now and then. I'll find you so you can fill me in. That's the way I want it."

"Okay," Charlie Bob said. "We'll do it your way."

Flank Steak was dissatisfied, but Charlie Bob seemed to have closed the subject, so he didn't say any more. They had gone just a short distance out of town when they spotted the campsite. The six men were there, already dismounted. One was stoking up the fire. A couple of others seemed to be busy with something. Slocum called a halt. They sat watching for a few minutes. Then Slocum said, "All right. You boys head on back. When you ride by the camp, don't slow down. Don't wave or say howdy. Just ride on."

"And you?" said Flank Steak.

"Don't worry about me. I'll be seeing you. Go on now."

The cowboys rode on. They did just as Slocum had told them. He watched the camp closely as Charlie Bob and Flank Steak passed it by. He could see some of the deputies stand up and watch, hands on their gun butts. When the two cowboys had ridden well by, the deputies relaxed again. Slocum had an idea what Comstock was up to, but he wasn't real sure about it. Hiring reinforcements and heading back toward Hangout just about cinched it though.

He figured that rather than bail out after the Snug T had whipped the LeDoux bunch, Comstock had run to the governor and told his side of the story. Then he had hired on a whole new crop of gunslingers for deputies. He was headed back for Hangout. His plan was most likely to take over where LeDoux had failed. Slocum figured that the first thing he would do would be to get the LeDoux spread in his own name. There were ways a crooked sheriff could do that. Then he would start lording it over the townfolk. He might lay off the Snug T for a while, but the time would come when he would be after them again. Slocum was sure of that.

He found himself a spot by the side of the road where he could watch the camp, and he settled down. The Appaloosa was grazing contentedly. Slocum watched as the six men milled around. It looked as if someone had made some coffee, and some of them were drinking it. They had laid out bedrolls for the night. A couple of the men had already stretched themselves out for the night. Comstock was one of those. A little later, all but one had gone to bed. Comstock was not totally stupid. He had seen that they left a guard. They would probably take turns at that job. Slocum waited a little longer. When they had all had time to go to sleep, all but the guard, he got up and walked over to his horse. He pulled the Winchester out of its scabbard and walked back to the side of the tree he had been sitting under before.

Leaning against the tree, he cranked a shell into the chamber of the Winchester and raised the gun to his shoulder. He took careful aim at the lone sentry. He did not even know who the man was. It was enough that he had gone to work for the murderous Comstock in the company of men like Slab and McCool. He squeezed the trigger. Then he hurried over to his horse and mounted up. He rode hard right past the camp, snapping off two more rounds that did nothing but make noise in the night. In a flash he was gone.

•   •   •

Riley Hill had been standing watch, and Slocum's slug had drilled him in the chest. He dropped dead instantly. The others all rose from their warm beds grabbing for weapons and getting to their feet. Comstock's feet got tangled in his blanket, and he fell forward on his face.

"God damn it," he said.

Then two more shots rang out, and everyone fell flat. Soon though the shots had stopped and the hoofbeats had faded away. The five remaining men held their guns ready and looked around, but there was no one to be seen.

"Who'd they get?" whispered Barker.

No one answered him immediately. Finally, Bacon said, "Riley was standing watch."

"They killed Riley," said Slab. "He's right over there. I can see him. They killed him dead."

Comstock finally stood up. He held a six-gun in his hand, but it was just hanging at his side by this time.

"It weren't no they," he said. "It was just one man. It was that goddamned Slocum. He done it, and he's gone now. You can all get up. There won't be no more shooting tonight. He's long gone."

Slab stood up slowly, looking around. Finally he faced Comstock. "Well, what the hell was he up to? Why kill Riley? We ain't done nothing to him. Not yet."

"He knows I'm after him," said Comstock. "He's fighting a war."

"Well, by God," said Slab, "we'll give him one."

"If we can find the son of a bitch," said McCool. "How the hell do we find him, Comstock?"

"He's been with the Snug T outfit," Comstock said. "That's where we'll start."

"And if he ain't there no more?" said Bacon.

"Then we'll comb the countryside," Comstock said. "We'll check every ranch, every line shack, every place where a man could make a camp. We'll find the bastard all right."

"And when we find him?" Barker said.

"Whoever finds him," said Comstock, "kill him. Kill him dead. There'll be a big bonus for that man."

"I hope it's me," said McCool. "If I can just get him in my sights, he'll be a dead man all right."

"You better hope he don't get you in his sights," said Slab. "God damn it, I can't sleep here tonight. Not now. I'll be thinking about that damn Slocum taking another shot at us from somewhere out there."

"He won't be back tonight," said Comstock, but his voice betrayed him. He no longer quite believed what he was saying. Slocum could have ridden ahead a ways and then turned around. He could be heading back for the camp at any time. He could be planning to take another potshot. No telling who he would drop the next time.

"I can't stay here, Comstock," said Slab.

"Me neither," said McCool.

"Ah, hell," Comstock said. "Let's mount up and go back into town. I'll get us some rooms for the night."

Ahead on the road, Slocum moved leisurely toward Hangout. He was trying to figure his next move. He could spend the night, what was left of it, in Hangout and be there when Comstock and his bullies arrived in the morning. It would be late morning, maybe even noon, by the time they got there. He could maybe pick off another one or two and then hightail it out of town. It would be risky though. It might be a foolish move. He decided against it. He already knew that he would not go back to the Snug T. He wanted to dissociate himself from that place, draw attention away from it. He did not want Comstock to bother the Snug T outfit anymore.

When Comstock and his gang got back into the capital, they went straight into the nearest saloon. Comstock had forgotten about his determination to get an early start, and they all felt like they needed a drink. Comstock got a bottle and five glasses, and they sat down at a table. The sheriff poured a round of stiff drinks. He looked at Slab.

"The governor authorized me to hire on eight new deputies," he said. "I found you men and thought that would be enough, but now Slocum's done killed one of you. Now I have only four deputies. Slab, I need four more men. Four more good men. Do you know where I can find them?"

Slab took a drink. He put down his glass and scratched his head, looking thoughtful.

"I think maybe I can come up with four more men, Comstock," he said. "It'll take some time. We won't be headed out of here early in the morning."

"Hell," said Comstock, "I've done give up on that notion. How long do you think it'll take you?"

"Well, two of them's in jail."

"How serious is the charge?"

"Just rowdiness."

"We can get them out easy enough," said Comstock. "What about the other two?"

"I'm pretty sure they're in town, but I ain't exactly sure just where. That's what'll take some time. Hunting them up."

"Are you sure these men will go with us?"

"When I tell them the setup," said Slab, "they'll go along."

"Good. We'll get after it first thing in the morning. Right now, I'm going to find us some rooms."

# 12

Slocum made it back to the Snug T all right. He wanted to let Chaney and Pearlie know what he was up to so they wouldn't be too worried about him. Well, they might worry, but at least they wouldn't be watching for his return all the time. It was early morning. He had been riding all night. He came up to the ranch house just in time to see Chaney come out the door. It was pretty obvious. He knew what had been going on in there overnight all right. He was a little jealous, too. He stopped his big Appaloosa just in front of the porch and howdied Chaney.

"Slocum," said Chaney. "We were wondering about you."

"Well, Comstock and them beat us to the governor's place, and it looks like the governor give him the go-ahead to hire on more deputies. It sure don't look like he's fixing to run off, Al. It looks more like he's fixing to take over where LeDoux left off."

"Damn," said Chaney. "Well, by God, we'll be ready for him."

"That's a good idea," said Slocum. "Stay ready, but don't start nothing. He's got the governor on his side. Leave it up to me. At least for now. I ain't going to be hanging around the ranch."

"What the hell will you do?"

"It's best you don't know. That's all I come to tell you."

Slocum touched the brim of his hat and turned his horse to ride off.

"Slocum," said Chaney, "hold on a minute."

Slocum continued riding. He called out over his shoulder, "Be seeing you."

Just then Pearlie came out onto the porch. "What's going on, Al?" she said.

"That's Slocum riding off," he said.

"I can see that. What did he say?"

"Comstock's been to see the governor, and he's hired on more guns. Slocum said for us not to start anything but to stay ready. He said leave it all up to him. He said he won't be around the ranch."

"What's he going to do?"

"He said we'd be better off we didn't know."

"Hell, Al," said Pearlie, "you know what that means."

"I guess so."

"He's going to set himself up as an outlaw. We can't let him do that."

"I don't see how we can stop him. You know, he liked your uncle an awful lot, and it was Comstock that done the killing."

"I know that, Al, but we've got to do something about it. Why didn't Flank Steak and Charlie Bob tell us about this?"

"They told us all they knew, Pearlie. Slocum sent them on back. It ain't their fault."

"I'm going to the capital," Pearlie said.

"Not by yourself."

"You can't go. You've got to watch things here."

"Well, you'll have to take along a couple of hands then. You can't go by yourself."

"All right," Pearlie said. "You pick out a couple of the boys. We'll get started right away."

Slab led Comstock and the other new deputies around the capital, moving from one saloon to another until he saw the two men he was looking for. They were standing at the bar drinking whiskey. "There they are, Mr. Comstock," he said.

He walked over to where the two men stood. Comstock and the others followed.

"Howdy, boys," Slab said.

The two men both looked at him. They were rough-looking bastards all right.

"Howdy, Slab," said one. He nodded toward Comstock, whose badge was showing. "Who's your friend?"

"This here is Sheriff Comstock from over to Hangout," said Slab. "He's my new boss, and he's looking for four more men. You boys interested?"

"You pulling my leg, Slab?"

"No. It's a sweet setup. Be worth a lot of money. What do you say?"

The two looked at each other and nodded. "All right," said the first one. "Count us in."

"Good," said Slab. "Mr. Comstock, this is Green Johnson. This other feller is Hack McGuire. Boys, shake hands with Mr. Comstock. You already know these others here, don't you?"

"Yeah, we know them. How do you do, Mr. Comstock?"

Comstock left all of his new deputies except Slab in the saloon with a bottle of whiskey. He and Slab walked over to the jail. Inside, the U.S. marshal asked them what they wanted.

"You still got Spike Allen and Jess O'Brien in jail?" Slab asked.

"I got them."

"Can we get them out?"

"I'll pay any fine," said Comstock.

The marshal looked up at Comstock and saw the badge.

"I'm Sheriff Comstock from Hangout," Comstock said.

"What the hell do you want with—Oh, hell, never mind. You be taking them away from here?"

"We'll all be headed back to Hangout," Comstock said.

"Well, by God, you can have them and good riddance. No fine. I'll just go turn them loose. The quicker you get out of town with them the better."

•   •   •

Even though they had just returned from the same trip, Charlie Bob and Flank Steak insisted that they wanted to ride along with Pearlie. They felt like they were working with Slocum, even though he had sent them home. This way, at least they would still have their hands in the deal. They got fresh horses and mounted up to ride with their boss lady. As they rode along the main road to the capital, Charlie Bob said, "Ma'am, do you know what Slocum's up to?"

"He told Al that we're better off not knowing," she said, "and he said that he was staying away from the ranch. I think I can guess though."

"You think he's going on a killing spree against Comstock and them?"

"That's what I'm afraid of."

"Well, Comstock's done been to the governor. They'll write Slocum down an outlaw, and they'll hound him to his death."

"That's why I'm going to see the governor, Charlie Bob. My uncle and the governor were good friends, and the governor will remember me. I don't know what Comstock told him, but you can be sure it was a pack of lies. I mean to tell him the truth and set all this straight."

"I sure do hope he'll listen. After all, Comstock is the sheriff."

"He'll listen. I'll make him listen."

"Yes, ma'am," said Charlie Bob.

"Where do you think Comstock is right now?" said Flank Steak.

"I'd say he was back in Hangout," said Charlie Bob. "We passed them on the road, but he's had time now to get on into town."

"What about Slocum?"

"He came by the ranch this morning," said Pearlie. "Then he left. Your guess is good as anyone's."

Nor did Slocum have any idea that Comstock had gone back into the capital after he had shot that deputy out on the road. He thought that Comstock and his new deputies would be hitting Hangout anytime now. In spite of that, he rode into town to gather up some supplies. He had no idea how long he would be out on the prairie alone, and he did not want to run out of anything at an inconvenient time. He loaded up on trail food, coffee, cigars and .45 shells. They were good for both his Colt sidearm and his Winchester rifle. He had himself a cup of coffee, and then he decided that he might be pressing his luck. He mounted up and rode out of town, taking the road that led back toward the capital.

A few miles out of town, where the hills rose on one side of the road, he found a likely spot and rode up into the hills. Dismounting, he led his Appaloosa back a little farther, making sure that he was well out of sight and leaving him there with plenty of fresh grass to graze on. Then he went back down a little farther and found himself a comfortable spot where a clump of brush nestled up against a fair-sized boulder. From there he could be hidden and he could command a good view of the road below. He settled down to wait. His plan was simple. When Comstock and his deputies came along, he could drop one or two at least with well-placed shots from his Winchester. Then he could get away clean.

Pearlie and the two cowhands had just rounded a curve in the road when they saw Comstock riding toward them with eight men. They stopped. Charlie Bob and Flank Steak tensed, ready for anything. The sheriff and his men rode closer. Then they, too, stopped. Sitting side by side on their horses, they blocked the entire road.

"You going to let me by?" said Pearlie to Comstock.

"Where might you be headed?" Comstock said.

"That's my business."

"Well now, it might be mine, too."

"Last I heard, this was a free country. I can ride out anywhere I want without answering to anyone."

"Things has changed around here on account of all the recent violence. I just come from seeing the governor. We got new rules in these parts. Now you want to tell me where you're headed for?"

"No. I don't."

"Well, that's all right. This here road only goes to the capital. I reckon that's where you'd be headed. You just as well turn around and head back to Hangout or to your ranch. This road is officially closed."

"You can't do that," Pearlie said.

"It's done. Turn around and ride back or get yourself arrested."

"Miss Pearlie?" said Flank Steak.

Pearlie sat and stared at Comstock. She looked at the eight men with him. She and her two cowhands did not stand a chance against them.

"Never mind, boys," she said. "Let's turn back."

"That's being smart, missy," Comstock said.

Pearlie and her two hands turned their horses and raced away, anxious to put as much space between them and the Comstock bunch as possible. Comstock smirked and urged his own mount on ahead at a still leisurely pace with the other eight men following.

From his spot above the road, Slocum saw Pearlie and the cowboys ride by in a hurry. He wondered what they were up to, but he kept himself hidden. They looked to be all right. Maybe he'd find out later. It didn't take long. In a few more minutes, Comstock came riding by with his men. Slocum cranked a shell into the chamber of his Winchester and raised the rifle to his shoulder. He took his time. He considered sniping Comstock himself, but just as he was about to pull the trigger another of the riders moved up alongside the crooked sheriff to block the shot.

"Damn," snarled Slocum. He didn't have the time to wait for a better shot at Comstock. Someone else would have to do. He zeroed in on the rider who had blocked his shot and pulled the trigger.

Down on the road, Chester Barker flinched. His head bobbed and then dropped against his chest. His hands relaxed and turned loose of the reins, and he slowly slid off his horse, falling to the road on the right side.

"God damn," shouted Comstock, as he lashed at his horse and raced ahead. The rest of his gang did the same. Then another shot sounded, and Tod McCool fell dead. Comstock and the remaining six deputies continued on as fast as they could toward Hangout.

Up above, Slocum stood up and considered a third shot, but his targets had all moved too far ahead. It would have been useless. He lowered his rifle, turned and walked back to his waiting horse. He mounted up and made his way back down to the road to check on the two fallen men. They were both dead. He rode away, leaving them there in the road.

Back at the Snug T, Pearlie and the two hands sat on the big front porch of the ranch house. Pearlie was cursing. The two cowhands felt like it themselves, but neither one wanted to use such language in front of a lady.

"Damn," Pearlie snapped. "He had no right. The son of a bitch."

"We'd have fought them if you'd said so," said Flank Steak.

"Bull shit," said Pearlie. "There were nine of them. We'd all be dead."

"Yes, ma'am," said Flank Steak.

"So what'll we do now?" Charlie Bob asked.

"Well, we're not giving up," she said. "Where the hell is Al?"

"He's likely out on the range," Charlie Bob said. "You want me to go find him for you?"

"No. It might take you all day. We'll just wait a little longer."

"Yes, ma'am."

Pearlie stood up suddenly. "You two wait right here," she said. "I'll be right back."

She went into the house. Flank Steak rolled himself a cigarette and lit it.

"Hey," said Charlie Bob. "Here comes Al."

Chaney rode up to the porch with a surprised look on his

face. "What are you doing back here?" he said. "Where's Pearlie?"

The two told Chaney what had happened out on the road. "Miss Pearlie's just inside the house," Charlie Bob added. "She said she'd be right back. Told us to wait here."

Chaney dismounted and tied his horse to the rail in front of the porch. He walked up on the porch just as Pearlie came back out. She was carrying a large sack filled with something.

"What you got there?" Chaney asked.

"More provisions," she said. "We're leaving again. Did the boys tell you what happened?"

"Yeah. They told me. I ain't sure you'd ought to be going again."

"We won't go by way of the road," said Pearlie. "We'll go around the long way. It'll take about twice as long to get there. That's how come I got these extra provisions."

Chaney thought about arguing more with her, but he knew it would do no good.

"Well," he said, "shouldn't you ought to wait till the morning now? You've wasted away a lot of this day already."

"I want to get going just as soon as we can. Boys, get us three fresh horses."

"Yes, ma'am," said Charlie Bob. He jumped up and started down the porch, followed hard on his heels by Flank Steak. Chaney looked at Pearlie. He still wanted to argue, but he knew that it would not make any difference. He took her in his arms and held her close.

# 13

When Comstock arrived back in Hangout, he was down to six new deputies. He was visibly shaken by the recent events out on the road. He did not lead his new deputies to the office. Rather he led them straight to the Bird's Beak Saloon, ordered a bottle of whiskey and seven glasses delivered to a table and sat down like a sack of flour dropped in the chair. The deputies all grabbed chairs and sat at the table with him. In another moment the bottle and glasses were delivered, and Comstock grabbed the bottle with a shaking hand, uncorked it, and poured himself a drink. He shoved the bottle to his right, where Slab picked it up to pour and scooted it on around the table. They had two drinks each before anyone spoke up. The bold one turned out to be Art Bacon.

"You reckon that was that damn Slocum out yonder?" he said.

"Who the hell else?" said Comstock.

"Just thought I'd ask."

"Well, it was him all right. The son of a bitch."

Comstock downed another glass of whiskey in a greedy gulp.

"What are we going to do about him, Mr. Comstock?" said Slab.

"You got to find that bastard and kill him," said Comstock, pouring yet another drink. "That's the main thing I

100

hired you for. To kill Slocum. Remember, he's a wanted man. Dead or alive. I don't want him alive."

"Where do we look?"

"Anywhere," said Comstock. "Everywhere. Hell, there ain't no telling where he'll be holed up. I reckon we could start with the damned Snug T, but I don't really believe he'd be out there. It's a place to start though. The Snug T."

"That's the main ranch you're after, ain't it?" said Slab.

"That's later, on down the line. I mean to lay off of them for a spell. We got two things to do right now. Slocum's number one. The other one, I'll take care of myself, and that's to set up a sheriff's auction for the LeDoux property. I'll get to that right away."

Comstock poured himself another drink.

"We'll have to get around to collecting taxes here pretty soon, too," he said. "I'll draw you a map showing where all the ranches are located with the names of their owners and how much they got to pay wrote right on it. Say, that's an idea. You can get started on that right away tomorrow morning. That way you'll be riding all over the county to collect the taxes, and you can be scouting for Slocum at the same time. Don't forget that thousand-dollar bonus to the man that gets him."

"That's right in the front of my mind," said Slab.

Slocum rode into Hangout by one of the back roads. He made his way to the rear of the Bird's Beak, dismounted and climbed up to the roof of the saloon. The front facade made a perfect place for hiding out. He peered over the top edge of the facade and saw the horses tied down there in the street. He recognized the animals the sheriff and his gang had been riding. They'd be coming out sometime. He could afford to wait.

As it turned out, he didn't have to wait long. Someone in the Comstock crowd finally got some sense, for Green Johnson came out of the saloon to gather up the horses and take them to the stable. Slocum recognized him as one of the new deputies. Johnson loosed the reins of two of the horses. Slocum drew out his Colt. It wasn't a long shot and wouldn't be difficult at all. He thumbed back the hammer and stood up behind the facade. Extending his arm, he pointed at Johnson's chest. Then he pulled the trigger. Johnson jerked, staggered and fell to the ground dead. The two loose horses ran down the street. Slocum holstered the Colt and ran to the back of the building, where he jumped off the edge of the roof. Landing in the saddle, he spurred his Appaloosa out of town.

Inside the Bird's Beak, Comstock stiffened at the sound of the shot. "Slab," he said, "you better check that out."

"Art, Spike, come on with me," Slab said as he stood up from the table. The three men hurried out the front door of the Bird's Beak, and there in front, lying in a spreading pool of blood in the street, they saw Green Johnson.

"Somebody shot Green," said Bacon.

"No shit," said Slab.

All three men pulled out their revolvers. They looked up and down the street, but they could find no target. Finally they gave it up.

"You two gather up them horses and take them on down to the livery," said Slab. "I'm going in to tell Comstock what's happened out here. And, hey. Watch yourselves. We're down to just five of us now."

Slab went back through the batwing doors and across the table where Comstock waited nervously with Jess O'Brien and Hack McGuire.

"Someone shot Green out in the street," he said. "We didn't spot no one. I sent Art and Spike to gather up the horses and take them on down to the stable."

"Is Johnson dead?" said Comstock.

"Dearder'n hell," said Slab.

"Slocum," said Comstock.

"You think he'd hit us again so soon?" asked Slab.

"It wasn't anyone else," said Comstock. "It was Slocum. Get those men you sent to the stable and search this whole damn town. Take the other side of the street. Me and these two men here will take this side. Go on."

Slab hurried on out to meet up with Spike Allen and Art Bacon. Comstock downed his drink and stood up on wobbly legs. "Let's go," he said. O'Brien and McGuire stood up to follow him. Soon the sheriff and his deputies were bursting through every door on the street and rummaging through the place, checking every door inside, every back room. Spike Allen found his way to the second floor of the hotel. He kicked open each room door, causing a few shrieks, then made his way to the far end of the hall. There was a door that led outside. Allen opened it and stepped out onto a small landing. A flight of stairs led down to the alley. He was about to go back inside, when he happened to look off across the vast prairie that lay in that direction. He caught sight of Slocum riding like hell, already with a good head start. Allen knew that firing his six-gun would have been a foolish waste.

He went back inside and ran down the hallway, down the stairs, through the lobby and out into the street. He pointed his six-gun straight up into the air and fired three shots, yelling at the same time, "Comstock. Slab. I found him." In a couple of minutes Comstock and all of the remaining deputies were gathered around Allen in the street.

"I found him," Allen said.

"Where?" said Comstock.

"Hightailing it out of town. I could tell it was him on account of that spotty-ass horse he rides."

"Which direction, damn it?" said Comstock.

Allen pointed. "He was headed thataway. I seen him from the back side of the hotel. Crossing that wide prairie back there."

"Get your horses, men," said Comstock. "Hurry it up."

Soon the posse was riding after Slocum, although he had already disappeared from sight. They rode across the prairie in the direction Allen had seen him going. They rode hard, with little regard for their horses, until they at last came to the far edge, where thick woods grew.

"He must have went in there," said Slab.

"Yeah," said Allen, "but whereabouts?"

"Can any one of you dumbasses read sign?" said Comstock.

"I'm a fair hand," said Hack McGuire. He started riding along the edge of the woods slowly, studying the ground as he moved. At last he stopped and dismounted. He knelt to study the ground more closely. He was right at a place where the woods opened up some. A space almost like a path wound its dark way into the trees. McGuire stood up. "He went in here," he said.

"All right," said Comstock. "Let's get after him. Hack, you ride first in case you need to read any more sign."

McGuire mounted his horse and turned it into the dark path. Comstock followed immediately behind him, and Slab moved in next. They rode slowly. "Keep your eyes peeled, boys," said the sheriff. "The son of a bitch might try to dry-gulch us again." They continued on their way, McGuire watching the ground, and the others looking up and to both sides nervously. It was a long and slow ride, but they made it, not to the other side of the woods, but to the place where the hills rose up, the woods creeping up their sides. McGuire stopped, looking up the side of the hill in front of him.

"He went on up here," he said.

"Keep going," said Comstock.

The hillside was dotted with boulders, some few as high as a man's head, most about half that size or smaller, visible because the trees thinned out some as well. Still, Slocum was nowhere in sight. McGuire urged his mount cautiously up the hillside, and the rest followed him. He had gone about a fourth of the way up, when he stopped and dismounted again, kneeling and studying the ground. Comstock sat quietly for a couple of minutes before losing his patience.

"Well?" he said.

McGuire stood up. "I've lost his trail," he said. "It just petered out. This ground is too rocky. He could've gone in any direction from here. Hell, he could even have turned around and gone back down into them thick woods."

"I doubt that," Comstock said. "I say we keep moving straight ahead up to the top of the hill."

He kicked his horse in the sides and moved out around McGuire, taking the lead. The way grew steeper, and the sheriff's horse stepped in a bed of loose rocks. It neighed an alarm, tried to dig its hooves in, but slipped, dumping the sheriff unceremoniously onto the ground and sliding back into McGuire's horse. The men were shouting, and the horses were bleating. Soon all had been knocked over and slid a ways back down the hill. At last, Comstock managed to get on his feet. He got hold of his horse's reins and calmed the animal somewhat. Looking back behind, he waited until all of his men had done the same.

"Is anyone hurt?" he called out. Apparently no one was. "Lead your damn horses from here on," he said. "Let's get going."

They trudged their way to the top of the hill, and then they all sat down on the ground or on boulders, panting. They let their horses go to graze. Slab rolled a cigarette and lit it. Comstock took a bottle out of his pocket, took a drink and passed it around. McGuire was standing and studying the layout below. He saw no sign of Slocum. At last Comstock stood up. He walked over to McGuire.

"You see anything?" he said.

McGuire shook his head. "Not a damn thing, Mr. Comstock," he said.

Comstock studied the terrain for a spell: all hills and valleys and green trees and rocks and boulders.

"What's out there, Mr. Comstock?" said Slab, moving up to stand beside the sheriff.

"Aw, there's a few small ranches," said Comstock. "There's easier ways to get to them than the way we come. I don't hardly get out this far in this direction. No reason to till now. Hell, damn, I guess we've lost him. Let's see if we can't find a easier way back down this goddamned thing and get back to town."

•    •    •

Slocum had crossed the big hill and then moved into a valley on the other side. He had no idea what lay before him. He was only putting distance between himself and Comstock's gang. He decided that he had been pretty bold and might be pressing his luck. It seemed like a good idea to lay low for a few days, think about things, come up with a plan. He made his way across the valley and topped another rise. Then he carefully hid his horse and snugged himself down low to watch his backtrail. He saw the Comstock gang reach the top of the hill and stop to rest. Then he saw them turn around and go back the way they had come, apparently giving up the chase. Slocum got back on the big stallion and rode down into the next valley. He relaxed some, knowing that the posse had given up on him, at least for the time being.

Down in the valley, he found a clean, clear stream, and he stopped to let the Appaloosa drink and graze. He himself bent over the stream for a drink, and he found that the water was good. Then he found a thick tree, sat under it, leaned back against the trunk, took out a cigar and lit it. He decided that this was as good a spot for a camp as he was likely to come across, so he got up and unsaddled his horse. He rolled out his bedroll and then built a small fire. Digging into his stash, he found some food and some coffee, and he built himself a meal. It felt good to be out away from everyone, enjoying a meal and the quiet. When he had finished his meal, he settled down with another cup of coffee and another cigar. At last he crawled into his bedroll and went to sleep.

The stream wound its way through the valley and between the hills into another little valley beyond. There it bubbled its way along, close to a small, modest ranch house. A corral stood not far from the house, with a small barn at one end. To one side of the house stood a grove of apple trees. Farther along, cattle grazed contentedly. A wire fence kept them out of the yard around the house and corral. Inside the house, Molly Morrison was working late. She had a bushel of apples, and she was sitting at a table peeling them. She was planning to make a couple of pies and then to can apple butter with the rest of the apples. She would be up late. Even so, she would still have to rise early to get after her other chores.

Molly thought now and then of trying to sell her little place. It was almost too much for a woman by herself. She had been alone now for over a year, since her husband had been killed in an accident. She had never known exactly what had happened. Late one evening his horse had come back to the corral alone. She had saddled another horse and taken the riderless one with her, searching for her man. Sitting there, peeling her apples, she recalled that awful night. It had been about this same time. It had taken a while, but at last she had come across the body. His skull was cracked, and he had one broken arm. He was dead. He was at the base of a hill. Maybe the horse had lost its footing, and they had fallen. Or perhaps something had spooked the horse, and it had thrown him. She would never know.

She had loaded the body onto the horse and taken it back to the house. There she had laid it out and cleaned it up. She dressed it in the best clothes her husband had owned, and the next morning, she dug the grave and laid him to rest. She never bothered telling anyone. There was no one to tell. They had seldom gotten to town and had no real friends. Neither of them had any family they kept in touch with. Now and then, she thought that if something were to happen to her out there, no one would ever know, and no one would care.

She finished peeling and started slicing the apples. It was going to be a long night. The apples for the apple butter would have to be put on to boil. The pies would be done long before the apple butter. She did not usually stay up like this, but the apples would not keep for much longer. They had to be dealt with.

Outside at the fence, a calf ducked and scooted under the lowest wire. It began to graze. The grass was better on the wrong side of the fence. It grazed for a while and then it went to the stream for a drink. It began grazing again along the edge of the stream, slowly but surely moving away from the house and the fence and the rest of the cattle.

# 14

When Slocum woke up the following morning, the first thing he saw was the stray calf. He pulled on his boots and strapped on his Colt. Setting his hat firmly on his head, he stood up and strolled over toward the animal.

"What the hell are you doing over here, little fellow?" he said.

The calf bawled a response. Slocum walked a little closer. It bawled again and turned, running back a ways. Then it stopped and turned again to look back at Slocum. It bawled again.

"You seem to be a little far off from your mama," Slocum said. He looked around and figured that the creature had to have come from upstream. He hadn't seen anything down the other direction, no sign of a ranch of a herd of cattle. Well, he might as well try to find its home, but he couldn't get too close to it. He strolled over to his saddle and took the coiled lasso off. He had started walking slowly toward the calf, readying the lariat for use, when he stopped suddenly at the sound of an approaching horse. Quickly he freed his right hand and readied himself for anything that might be coming his way. Then from around a bend up ahead, a woman came riding toward him. She reined in a short distance away.

"What were you fixing to do with my calf, cowboy?" she said.

Slocum looked at the woman. She was maybe thirty, with long auburn hair. She'd had a hard life, and it showed, yet she was still a damn good-looker. She wore men's clothing, had a six-gun strapped on and a rifle in a saddle scabbard.

"She looked lost or strayed to me," he said. "I thought I'd try to find her home. Looks like I don't need to."

Molly Morrison believed the man's story. He had an honest look about him, although he also had the look of a man who had been in a good many fights and come out ahead on all of them. "Well," she said, "throw your loop on her." She dismounted as Slocum roped the calf. It started bawling in earnest then and kicking and jumping around. Molly walked over to Slocum and took the rope from him. Then she walked back to her horse and tied it to the saddle horn. Turning back to Slocum, she smiled, and Slocum liked the look of the pleasant expression.

"I'm Molly Morrison," she said, extending her hand.

Slocum took it in his own. "I'm called Slocum," he said.

"Just Slocum?"

"It's usually enough."

"You had your breakfast?" Molly asked.

"I just woke up and saw your calf," Slocum said.

"Why don't we take her home," she said, "and I'll fix you up some ham and eggs and a good pot of coffee."

"I sure won't turn down an offer like that," Slocum said. He saddled his Appaloosa, packed up quickly, and mounted, riding alongside Molly as she made her way back to the ranch house. Slocum watched as she shooed the calf back through the fence.

"She'll come right out of there again," he said. "Have you got any wire?"

"I've got some in the barn," she said. "Been meaning to patch that up. I just ain't got around to it yet."

"Why don't I do that for you while you whomp up that breakfast?"

"I'd call that more than fair," Molly said.

She showed Slocum where to put his horse so that it had water, oats and hay, and they unsaddled both animals. Then she showed him the wire and tools. Slocum took them up and headed back toward the weak spot in the fence. Molly went into the house. The fence patching job was an easy one that didn't take long in the doing. He put the rest of the wire and the tools back in the barn, washed up a bit in the water trough and walked to the house. He rapped on the door and opened it just a bit.

"Come on in," Molly said.

Slocum went in, and saw that Molly was already putting the food on the table. She poured him a cup of coffee and motioned for him to sit down. He sat and took a slurp of the coffee. It was good. Molly dished out the food and sat down. Slocum tied right in.

"What brings you way out here anyhow?" Molly asked suddenly. Then she added, "Course, maybe it ain't none of my business."

"Maybe it ain't," he said, "but I don't mind telling you. I'm running from the law." He looked across the table to get her reaction to that. She seemed to have tensed just a little.

"Anything bad?" she said.

"The sheriff murdered a friend of mine," he said. "I fought back."

She cocked her head and looked at him for a moment. "You come out of that damn Hangout?" she asked.

"How'd you guess?"

"I don't get into town often," she said, "but I've heard about how that LeDoux and his paid-for sheriff run things."

"LeDoux's not running anything anymore," he said. "I was working for the Snug T outfit when they killed Mr. Tyson. I was right there. Saw the whole thing. He wasn't even armed. Anyhow, we got to fighting back, and we wiped out that LeDoux bunch, but Comstock got to the governor first. He's accused me of all the killings. I got a few of his deputies, but then I decided I ought to get out for a spell."

"You're welcome here, Slocum," she said.

"Thanks. If you don't mind feeding me, I'll sleep in the barn and work for my keep for a spell."

"I don't mind," she said. "It's been lonesome out here the last year." She told Slocum the story about her husband, what had happened to him, and how she had been working the small operation alone ever since then. He looked at her and decided that she had the look of a woman who could do it all right.

"That's quite a job for a woman alone," he said. "From the looks of things, though, I'd say you've done a hell of a job—except for that little piece of fence."

She laughed at that, and he joined in the laughter. Then she poured them each a second cup of coffee. When they had finished, he helped her with the dishes. Then they went outside and saddled their horses again. She led the way out the back side of the corral into her pasture, and they rode out over it looking over her herd. They were sitting quietly watching the cattle graze at the far end of the pasture.

"Molly," Slocum said, "how'd you manage to keep out of the way of LeDoux and Comstock and that bunch all this time?"

"The only thing I can figure," she said, "is that they were too busy messing with the Snug T to bother with us out here. They probably figured that if they ever managed to take over the Snug T, they could come out this way and take us easy enough."

"Yeah," Slocum said. "That makes sense."

"I don't guess they ever knew that I was out here alone," she said. "I never bothered going into town to tell anyone what had happened out here. If they'd known that, they might have come out after me anyway. You know, this place would have made them a good base to operate from. They could've had men on both sides of the Snug T."

"By God," said Slocum, "they could have."

"We ought to be heading back," Molly said. "It'll be lunchtime by the time we get back."

"All right."

They rode back a different way from the way they had

gone out. They were on the other side of the small cattle herd and on the side of the pasture the stream ran through. They came across one cow that had waded into the stream and was hung up in some brush under the water. Molly threw a loop over her head and Slocum waded out into the stream to get her untangled from the brush. The cow bawled something fierce until she was loose. Then she came running out of the stream, grateful to be free once again. It took them a while to get Molly's rope off her neck. They made it the rest of the way without incident.

Once again, they put their horses away. Molly asked Slocum if he had some dry clothes. He said that he had fresh jeans and socks. That was all he needed. She told him to bring them along to the house. In the house, she said that he could use the bedroom to change. He went in there and pulled off his boots, socks and jeans. Then he put on the dry jeans and socks and carried his wet boots out into the main part of the house, setting them on the floor by the door. She invited him to come back to the table and sit, and she poured him another cup of coffee. After they had finished lunch, they went outside to sit in front of the house and drink another cup. Slocum lit a cigar. They made small talk for a while.

"Slocum," she said, "what do you aim to do?"

"I thought I'd lay low for a spell," he said. "Maybe let that Comstock gang think that I've skipped the country. Then I'll go back to finish them off."

"That could be dangerous," she said.

"It'll be dangerous for them," Slocum said. "It's just something I've got to do."

"But if Comstock already got to the governor," Molly said, "you'll likely be a wanted man for the rest of your life. The best of it might be that you'll have to get out of this territory and stay out—for good."

"Yeah," he said. "I've thought about that. Well, it ain't the first time I've been running from the law. It likely won't be the last."

"You're a rare breed, Slocum," she said.

"I don't know about that. Say, that wood pile looks like it could use a little work," he said.

"Well, yeah. It could."

"I'll just get after it. That is, unless you've got something more pressing."

"The wood pile will do just fine," she said.

Slocum got up and went to work. He picked up the ax and set to splitting logs. Molly went back into the house for a short while. Then she came back out and walked to the barn. Slocum caught a glimpse of her now and then, shoveling manure, pitching hay. When he had at last gotten all the wood split, he walked to the barn to give her a hand. Soon they had everything done out there. They made sure the horses had enough food. The corral gate, though still functioning, was in need of repair, and Slocum took care of that little chore. At last they stopped. They were leaning on the corral fence, catching their wind.

"You're pretty handy around a ranch," Molly said.

"I've done my share of ranch work," he said.

"Don't take offence," she said, "but I'd have said that you had more the look of a gunfighter about you."

"Well," he said, "I reckon I've done plenty of that, too. I don't go looking for trouble, Molly, but it does seem to follow me around. And when it comes, I don't run from it."

"I bet you don't," she said. "Let's go back to the house. I'm about to starve. How about you?"

"I could eat a fair share."

They walked to the house and went inside, and Molly started right to work on supper. In a while, they were finished with it and with the dishes. Molly told Slocum that she needed a bath. They drew water from the well, heated it on the stove and filled up a large washtub there on the kitchen floor. Slocum went back outside. He smoked a cigar and sat looking over the small ranch. He was thinking that he would wash himself off some in the trough again and then go to the barn for the night. Molly opened the door and looked out. Her hair was wrapped in a towel, and she had nothing on except a long-tailed shirt.

"Slocum," she said, "you want the bath?"

"Oh, no, ma'am," he said. "Thanks just the same. I'll make do out here."

"Come on," she said. "I'll leave you alone. I need to gather up some eggs anyway."

"Well, if you're sure I won't be no bother," he said. "It would feel good."

"Come on and help yourself," she said.

Slocum went into the kitchen. The same bathwater that Molly had used was still in the tub. He tested it and found it still warm. He pulled off his shirt and tossed it over the back of a chair. Then he sat down to pull off his boots. Molly went out the front door and called back as she was going, "Take your time. I'll be out here for a while."

When Slocum had settled into the warm water, he couldn't help his thoughts from straying. He was sitting naked in the same tub, in the same water, that Molly had been in just minutes before. He picked up the soap and rubbed it over his body, thinking all the while how it had just been rubbed all over hers. She was a beautiful woman, for one of her age who had lived through what she had lived through. And she was nice and pleasant. She was easy to work with— or for. He tried to decide if he was working for her or with her. If he was working for her, he was working for his meals and a roof to sleep under. Well, hell, he had worked for a lot less. And her company was good. He had enjoyed this first day on her ranch. He thought about how easy it would be to just forget the outside world and settle down here with Molly. But then he thought that he had tried things like that before, and his past had always caught up with him somehow. There was just no use thinking thoughts like that.

He rubbed the soap all over his body and in his hair, and then he rinsed himself off the best he could. He reached for a towel, stood up and dried himself. Then he pulled on his jeans and his boots. He walked to the front door and stepped outside. Molly was making her way back to the house.

"Where do you want to throw out the water?" he asked.

"Oh, we'll just toss it out the back door," she said.

They both went back in, and together they dragged the tub of water to the back door and tossed the water out. Then Molly had Slocum draw another bucket up from the well and used it to rinse out the tub. They went back inside, and Slocum started to gather up his things.

"Say," Molly said, "I've got a bottle of good whiskey in here. It's been here for some time. I don't often drink any. Would you like a shot?"

"That does sound real good," he said.

Molly went to a cabinet for the bottle, got a couple of glasses and brought them to the table. She poured two drinks and gave one to Slocum. He lifted his glass to her as for a toast. Then he took a sip.

"That's mighty good," he said.

Molly sipped from her glass and winced as she swallowed. "Yeah," she said. They both laughed at that. Slocum suddenly felt self-conscious, and he reached for his shirt and pulled it on.

"Sorry, ma'am," he said, "I shouldn't have been—"

"Oh, that's all right, Slocum," she said. "One thing though. I wish you'd call me Molly."

"All right, Molly."

He finished his drink and stood up. "Thanks for the whiskey," he said. "I guess I'll be turning in."

He headed for the door and leaned over to pick up his boots.

"Slocum," she said.

He turned back toward her. "Yeah?"

"You don't have to sleep in the barn."

# 15

Slocum dropped the bar in place to keep any unwanted visitors out, although the chances of anyone showing up out there in that lonesome spot were remote. He dropped his gear to the floor and turned to face Molly. She was standing by the table, looking at him with longing, and her total appearance was incredibly seductive. At the same time she seemed particularly vulnerable, a woman just over a year widowed, just over a year alone, working hard to maintain on a hardscrabble ranch far away from any other human beings. Slocum's feelings toward this woman were mixed. They were troubling.

He walked over to her and put his hands on her shoulders, looking her in the eyes, but she almost immediately reached around him and pressed herself against him, nestling her head against his chest. He put his arms around her and squeezed her close to him. "Molly," he said, but she interrupted him.

"I know, Slocum," she said. "You're only here for a short time. There can't be anything lasting in this. It's all right. I understand that."

She moved back just enough to lift her face and look at him. Their lips met in a tender kiss. They parted, and then they kissed again, this time more passionately, lips parting, tongues probing. At the same time, they squeezed one another's bodies closer together, holding each other as if for dear life. At last they parted again, and Molly turned sideways, keeping one arm around Slocum and one of his arms around her shoulder, and walked toward the bedroom. He moved along with her. As they stepped into the bedroom, he asked her, "Are you real sure about this, Molly?"

"I told you, didn't I?" she said. She broke loose from him and sat on the edge of the bed, bending over to pull off her boots. Slocum began to undress. Soon, both naked, they faced each other in the dim light. One lamp still burned in the main room, some of its illumination seeping through the bedroom door. As Molly lay back on the bed, Slocum moved toward her. He reached the bed and put one knee on it, as she allowed her legs to fall apart and reveal the dark joy that was nestled between them. Slocum crawled in beside her. His cock was already growing.

As he rolled over on his left side to face her, his right hand reached for one soft but firm breast. He began to knead it lovingly. She moaned with pleasure and anticipation, and reached down with one hand between his legs. She stroked his balls, and then slid her hand up just a bit higher to grasp his now stiff rod. She gripped it hard, and it bucked in her hand. "Oh," she moaned, pulling him toward her, on top of her, by his handle. He rolled between her legs and allowed her to guide the greedy thing into just the right spot. It was wet and warm and ready, and Slocum thrust deep. She moaned again, this time more loudly and with greater pleasure.

Their bodies knit together, and their movements were in perfect harmony, each of her upward thrusts corresponding with one of his downward jabs. Slocum got a hand on each of her lovely breasts and kissed her as they continued humping. At last the pressure was too much for him, and he gushed forth into her body. In another moment, he rolled off her and lay quietly by her side.

"That was nice, Slocum," she said. "It was gentle. That was good for the first time. The next one can be wilder and rougher."

•   •   •

Slab walked into Comstock's office. The potbellied sheriff was sitting behind his desk. He looked up as the deputy slammed the door behind himself. "Morning, Mr. Comstock," said Slab.

"Howdy," said Comstock. "Something on your mind?"

"Yeah," said Slab. "We ain't been doing much the last few days. Ever since Slocum killed poor ole Green Johnson, he ain't showed himself again. We been wondering if he skipped the damn county or something."

"He might have," said Comstock, "but I wouldn't count on it. He could show up and take a potshot at me or you or anyone at just any time. I'd keep an eagle eye out for him, and tell the others to do the same."

"We been thinking about that thousand-dollar bounty you put on him, too," Slab said. "We'd kind of like to be out trying for it."

Comstock leaned back in his chair and studied Slab for a moment. "You're right," he said. "It's about time. Tell you what. I've drawn up that map I told you about." He picked up a piece of paper from his desk and shoved it across at Slab. Slab took it up to study. "I think it's clear enough. You see where the road runs right through Hangout going north and south? The other roads and trails are all marked clear. It shows you the locations of all the ranches and farms all around here."

"Yeah," said Slab. "It's clear enough."

"I've got some papers all drawed up, too, showing the amount of taxes that each landowner owes, and I've got another paper here that says we got a right to search any house in the county for the fugitive Slocum. Let's combine these here two duties. What do you say?"

"You mean we'll go out collecting taxes and be hunting Slocum at the same time," Slab said.

"That's right."

"I'll go round up the boys right now."

"Have them get my horse ready, too," said Comstock. "I'll ride out with you, at least for a while. The first stop will be the Snug T."

• • •

Charlie Bob and Flank Steak rode alongside Pearlie in the backcountry, taking the long way around to the capital, avoiding the main road where Comstock's men might intercept them again. As they moved up a rugged path on the side of a steep hill, Flank Steak said, "It sure is going to take us a while to get over there going this here way."

"We got no choice, Flank Steak," said Pearlie. "It's either this or fight an army, and I don't see any sense in fighting just now. We got to get things straight with the governor first."

"We know that, ma'am," said Charlie Bob. "Flank Steak's just grousing on account of he likes to grouse."

"Aw, I didn't mean it to sound like that," Flank Steak said. "I was just talking to hear my own voice, I reckon."

"That's all right," said Pearlie. "And you were right about it anyhow. It is going to take us a while going this way."

When Comstock and his five deputies came riding up, a lone cowhand stood watch at the main gate that led onto the Snug T Ranch. He looked nervous when he saw who it was approaching. Comstock hauled back on his reins just in the gateway. "We got business with your boss," he said.

"Is there going to be any trouble?" the cowhand said.

"No trouble," said Comstock. "Move aside."

The cowhand moved and said, "Well, I guess you can check at the ranch house." He knew that Pearlie was gone, but he did not want to give away that information. Comstock and the others moved on through and headed down the lane toward the house.

Al Chaney was at the corral about to saddle a horse when he saw the gang riding up. He threw the saddle across the fence and walked to the front porch to meet them. Comstock halted his bunch just in front of the porch.

"What business you got here, Comstock?" said Chaney. He wished that he had more men around him. He was edgy.

"I need to see your boss lady," Comstock said.

"Well, she ain't here just now," Chaney said.

"Where might she be at?" said the sheriff.

"Well, uh, I can't rightly say," said Comstock hesitantly. "She rode out early this morning to check on some of the cattle, but I ain't sure just what direction she went in. She won't likely be back here till late."

"Now, that's just a bit troubling," said Comstock, "on account of we're out collecting overdue taxes." He reached into an inside pocket of his coat and drew out a piece of folded paper. "This here paper shows that she owes the county three hundred dollars."

"I don't know anything about that," Chaney said. "Could it wait till I see her again? We could bring it into town to you in a day or two."

"It's already overdue," Comstock said. "If it ain't paid today, I won't have no choice but to take over the ranch and call for an auction. That's the law."

Chaney couldn't think of any other response. He did not want Pearlie to come home to find her ranch on the block. "Maybe I can find the cash," he said. "Wait here."

"I think we'll just go in with you," Comstock said, dismounting. The others did the same. Chaney hesitated.

"I'll be right back with it," he said.

"It ain't that, Al," said Comstock. "I got me another paper here that says I can search the house." He pulled it out of his pocket to show to Chaney. "You see, we're hunting the fugitive killer Slocum. He used to work here for you, didn't he?"

"Yeah," Chaney said. "Well, he worked for Mr. Tyson. He was a particular favorite of Mr. Tyson's. Now that Mr. Tyson's gone, well, so is Slocum."

"I believe you," said Comstock, "but I reckon we'll still have to take a look for our own selves. It just makes sense, now don't it."

The six crooked lawmen followed Chaney into the house, and Comstock pointed the other five in different directions to search the place. He stayed in the room with Chaney while Chaney went to get the money. Chaney was nervous about that. He didn't really want the sheriff to see where the money was kept, but he seemed not to have a choice in the matter. He was in no shape to chance a fight, and besides that, he knew that Pearlie did not want a fight. Not just yet. He got the cash box out of a drawer and took out three hundred dollars. Comstock reached for it.

"You going to give me a receipt for this, aren't you?" Chaney said.

"Oh, yeah. Sure. You got a piece of paper and a pencil?"

Chaney produced them, and Comstock scrawled something on the paper. The deputies were returning from the other rooms.

"No one here," said Slab.

Comstock made sure they all saw the money as he tucked it into a pocket.

"Okay," he said. "Let's go check the barn and the bunkhouse."

The sheriff's gang left the Snug T having seen no sign of Slocum or of Slocum's big Appaloosa. Chaney stood and watched them ride away, his jaws tightened in anger. Three hundred dollars was a lot of money. Furthermore, it was not even his money to give away. He hated having been forced to make that decision, but he had not seen any way around it. He thought that Comstock should have had to give Pearlie some notice before taking over her ranch. But he had said the money had to be paid. It was already overdue. And Chaney knew nothing about the taxes on the property.

"Son of a bitch," he said.

Comstock and his bunch hit three more ranches that day. They were smaller than the Snug T. He only charged one two hundred dollars and the other one hundred and fifty, but the owner of the last ranch said he did not even have that. Comstock gave him a week to clear out. The gang rode back into Hangout feeling as if they'd had a long and tiring workday. They went into the sheriff's office, where Comstock put all the cash out on his desk: five hundred dollars. He knew there would be more coming, and he felt like he needed to seem particularly generous just then. He handed each of the deputies a hundred dollars. Slab looked at him with curiosity.

"You didn't keep any for yourself," he said.

"That's all right," said Comstock. "There'll be more, and besides that, you boys have earned it."

The five deputies thanked Comstock profusely and started out the door grinning, counting their money or stuffing it into their pockets.

"Hold on just a minute," Comstock said. They stopped and looked back at him.

"I don't want you leaving them horses standing out there at the rail in your hurry to get over to the Bird's Beak. You take them all down to the stable, mine included, and get them took proper care of before you go to drinking up all that money I just give you."

The deputies all laughed, and Slab said, "I'll see they do it, Mr. Comstock."

"And don't stay up too late or get too drunk," Comstock said, " 'cause we're going out for more taxes in the morning."

"And more Slocum hunting," said Slab.

"That, too. A thousand dollars. Remember?"

"We ain't forgetting that, Mr. Comstock. No, sir."

It was late as Pearlie and her two cowhands were moving down the side of a steep hill. It was about time to be making a camp for the evening, but the steep hillside was no place for a camp. They would have to keep moving till they found a suitable place. Charlie Bob was leading the way, moving slowly and cautiously, with Pearlie next and Flank Steak taking up the rear. Suddenly Pearlie's horse gave a frightened neigh and tried to rear on its hind legs. It lost its footing and fell to one side, pinning Pearlie's leg underneath it. It screamed and flailed, trying to get back to its feet, but it was having no luck. All it was doing was wiggling all of its tremendous weight on Pearlie's leg. Pearlie winced with the pain. Charlie Bob and Flank Steak both managed to dismount, but they both had a time calming their own horses, frightened by the terrifying scene that was taking place there between them. At last, Flank Steak got his horse calmed enough to leave him alone, and he hurried to Pearlie's side.

He made a couple of false moves in an attempt to get the fallen horse to its feet again, but then he realized that it was no use. The animal had a broken leg. About then, Charlie Bob calmed his own horse and turned to help. He stopped when he saw the look on Flank Steak's face.

"We ain't going to get him up," said Flank Steak. "His leg's broke."

"Damn," said Charlie Bob.

"Shoot him," said Pearlie.

"Well, then," said Flank Steak, "how'll we get him up off of you?"

"Just shoot the poor thing," said Pearlie. "Then we'll talk about it."

Charlie Bob jerked out his six-gun and fired one well-placed shot that killed the horse immediately. He stood staring for a moment after. Then he put the gun away. He looked around till he saw a long piece of fallen wood, like a long pole. He ran over to get it. Then he looked for a rock about the right size.

"Help me with this," he said to Flank Steak.

They moved the rock near the body of the horse, and Charlie Bob laid the pole across it and poked one end underneath the horse, as close as he dared to Pearlie's leg.

"Miss Pearlie," he said. "Is your leg busted, do you think?"

"I don't think so," Pearlie said. "You won't have to shoot me."

Charlie Bob pried with the pole, possibly making a little difference, while Flank Steak pulled Pearlie by her shoulders. She put her free foot against the saddle and pushed as hard as she could. At last she came free. She stood up slowly and carefully, testing the leg. It was sore, but it worked.

"I'm all right," she said. "Let's get on down this damn hill. We'll walk your horses the rest of the way down."

# 16

Comstock and his gang swooped down on P.J. Merchand's place. It was a one-horse operation, not much of a spread, but it was all that Merchand had. He had been struggling with the place for the last five years trying to eke out a living. He owed money at the bank and at the general store in Hangout. He did not drink and did not smoke. It was not that he was a prude. He just couldn't afford the habits. Comstock had come by a week ago demanding one hundred and fifty dollars for taxes. Of course, Merchand had said that he didn't have it. Comstock had given him a week to clear out. Merchand had not taken him seriously. After all, it was his home.

When he saw the gang coming, Merchand dropped his pitchfork and ran for the house, a small one-room shack. He ran inside, shut and bolted the door, then picked up a rifle that stood just inside and cranked a shell into its chamber. Then he moved to the nearest window, just to the right of the door. There was no glass on the window, just wooden shutters. Merchand threw open one of the shutters and poked the barrel of the rifle out the window. Just about then, Comstock and the gang hauled up in front of the house.

"Merchand," Comstock called out. "You in there?"

Slab leaned over and patted Comstock's shoulder. Comstock looked at him, and Slab gestured toward the window from which the rifle barrel protruded.

"He's in there all right," Slab said.

"Oh yeah," said Comstock. "I see." Then he yelled out in full voice again, "Merchand, we know you're in there. You'd best put down that rifle and come on out."

"I ain't doing it," said Merchand. "This is my home, and I ain't letting you throw me out."

"It's all been done legal and proper," Comstock said. "It ain't yours no more. The county has done took it over. Your time is up. I gave you a week to pack up and get out. Now you just got to get."

"Be damned if I will," shouted Merchand, and he fired a shot that nicked Comstock's right ear.

"Yow. Damn," yelped Comstock, grabbing for his ear and getting a handful of blood. His horse screamed at the same time and reared, unseating the sheriff, who was unceremoniously dumped flat on his back on the hard packed dirt. "Oof," he said with his landing, and the air was all knocked from his lungs.

The five deputies all pulled six-guns and began firing at the window, but Merchand had slammed the shutter closed and ducked away. Their shots peppered and splintered the shutter, eventually causing it to swing wide open again, but Merchand was not there. He had moved to a different window on the other side of the door. Opening one of those shutters just a tiny bit, he poked his rifle out that window and took aim at the best target he could find. Squeezing the trigger, he fired off a shot that tore into Jess's throat. A horrible gurgling sound came out with the gushing blood. O'Brien slumped dead over his horse's neck, and the confused animal began running in circles, getting in the way of the other four deputies.

Merchand was about to fire again, but he was having trouble coming up with a good target through the tiny slit he had left himself in the window. Outside, the four deputies dismounted hurriedly when O'Brien was hit. They scattered around the yard, each searching for his own cover. Slab and Bacon had the foresight to grab rifles before leaping out of their saddles. The other two were still armed with just their six-guns. Merchand lost sight of them all. He ducked low and ran back to the other window, which was wide open. Looking out, he fired a shot that whistled close by the side of Spike Allen's head.

By this time, Comstock, still flat on his back, had managed to catch his breath, but with bullets flying all around, he was afraid to try to get up. He was also afraid to let Merchand know that he had not been killed. He lay still there where he had fallen, trying not to wince and flinch with the sound of each shot.

Pearlie was riding in Flank Steak's saddle with Flank Steak sitting behind. They were off the mountain and moving across flat and open prairie. They figured that with a little luck, they might make the capital by dark that evening. But Pearlie figured also that if it was that late when they arrived, she would have to wait until morning to try to see the governor. They still had a pretty good ride ahead of them, and she did not want to take a chance on ruining either of their two remaining horses.

"Boys," she said, "let's haul here and rest the horses."

They stopped and dismounted, allowing the horses to graze with trailing reins. Flank Steak and Charlie Bob poured water from their canteens into their hats and gave it to their horses to drink. Pearlie sat down on the ground with a long sigh. Flank Steak rolled himself a cigarette and lit it. He offered the makings to Charlie Bob, but Charlie Bob turned them down. Flank Steak dropped to his haunches not far from where Pearlie sat.

"We ought to hit the capital by dark," Flank Steak said.

"That's what I figure," said Pearlie.

"Will you try to see the governor tonight?" Charlie Bob asked.

"I don't think so," she said. "I'll see when we get there, but most likely I'll wait till morning. It's usually not a good idea to bother someone who's already gone home from work. Especially if you want to get something from him."

"I guess you're right there," said Charlie Bob.

"Sure you don't want a smoke?" said Flank Steak.

"No, thanks," said Charlie Bob. Then back again to Pearlie, he said, "So you think we'll head back for the ranch tomorrow?"

"Probably," she said. "It depends on how soon I get in to see the governor though. We'll buy me another horse over there, and I'll tell you one more thing. We'll go back to the Snug T by the main road. Comstock or no Comstock."

"Yes, ma'am," said Charlie Bob.

Pearlie decided that they had rested the horses long enough, so they got up to resume their journey. This time she got into Charlie Bob's saddle, and Charlie Bob got on behind.

Al Chaney had set the ranch hands to work, leaving a few to guard the place, and then taken one man with him for a ride into Hangout. There were a few things they needed from town. If he had thought that they could get along without them, he'd have let it wait, but you can't work a bunch of cowhands without coffee, and they were just about out. They were riding the road toward town when they heard shots ahead.

"Sounds like they're coming from P.J.'s place," said the cowhand.

"Come on," said Chaney. "Let's ride up around that bend yonder and then hide in the rocks."

They rode hard till they came to the rocks Chaney had mentioned, and then they rode their horses back behind them and dismounted. Taking their rifles with them, they hurried down close to the road and ducked behind some smaller rocks.

"That's Comstock's crew," said Chaney.

"What the hell're they up to?" said the cowboy.

"Whatever it is, it's no good," Chaney said. "Let's give ole P.J. a hand."

"Do we shoot to kill?"

Chaney thought quickly about how Pearlie had said they did not want a shooting war, not yet. "Let's see if we can just scare them off," he said. The two started firing rapidly, their shots hitting here and there on the ground near the horses' hooves, causing the animals to rear and dance about. Art Bacon nearly lost his seat.

"Hey," he shouted. "Who the hell is that?"

"God damned if I know," said Slab. "Let's get the hell out of here."

That last remark frightened Comstock to his feet. He looked around frantically for his horse, finally spotting it back toward the road still running loose and confused. He ran for it as hard as he could go. The four remaining deputies were fighting with their own spooked mounts, trying to get them to calm down enough to turn toward the road and get moving back toward Hangout. Finally, the four headed for the road. Comstock had reached his own horse, only to have it bolt away from him again. Inside the house, Merchand at first stopped firing and looked out with curiosity to try to figure out what was going on. Then he started to laugh. Comstock at last managed to get hold of his horse. He grabbed the horn and got his foot into the stirrup, and Merchand fired a shot that kicked up dirt between the creature's front legs. The horse bolted again, dragging Comstock out into the road. The last anyone saw of the sheriff, he was still hanging onto the saddlehorn, running for dear life alongside the unmanageable animal.

Chaney and his puncher waited till the sheriff and his deputies had gone past them on their cowardly way back to Hangout. Then they got their horses and rode up to Merchand's house. He saw them coming and stepped out to meet them. He was still laughing. Chaney and the puncher dismounted. When Merchand stopped laughing, Chaney said, "What was that all about?"

"That goddamned Comstock," Merchand said. "He come out here a week ago and demanded a hundred and fifty dollars from me. Taxes, he said. I told him I didn't have no money, so he said I had a week to clear out. The county's taking over, he said. Sure enough, the week's over today, and he come back with them new deputies of his to drive me off. Well, I don't mean to be driv off. That's all."

"I see you dropped one of them," the cowhand said.

"And I'll drop the rest if they come back."

"They'll be back, P.J.," Chaney said. "You know Comstock ain't going to just let this go."

"I'll be waiting for the bastards," said Merchand.

"You might not be so lucky next time. You know, we come along at just the right time."

"Yeah? Well, they might not be so lucky either. You ever think of that?"

"What if I was to send a couple of boys out here to watch with you just in case they come back?"

"Ah, I don't know."

"I'll send provisions along with them so they don't eat you out of house and home. You know, P.J., this ain't just your fight. He'll be after the Snug T before long if we let him keep getting away with this."

"Well, all right, Al. Just as long as it ain't charity."

"You can be sure it ain't," said Chaney. "Hell, I had to pay him three hundred myself just because Pearlie said she didn't want no fighting. Not yet. But if they come out here to fight you, and a couple of my boys happen to be here, well, it won't be their fault. They won't have started the fight."

"You put it that way," said Merchand, "I'll be glad to have them."

Comstock and the four deputies made it into Hangout all right, and they went straight to the Bird's Beak Saloon. Inside, Comstock got a bottle and five glasses, and they all went to a table at the back of the room. They had a drink before any one of them said a word.

"Was that Slocum?" said Slab.

"No," said Comstock. "I don't think so. Slocum would've killed someone. The son of a bitch. I think he's left the fucking county. Besides that, there was more than one of them. Three or four at least from the way they was shooting at us."

"Well then who the hell was it?"

"I'm damned if I know. I'd think it was those damn Snug T bastards, but I don't think they want to be fighting just now. They might though. You know, we caught them on the way to the capital the other day."

"So what do we do about them?"

"I'm thinking on it."

Spike Allen downed his drink and stood up. "I think I'll go out and take care of the horses," he said.

"Yeah. That's a good idea," Comstock said.

Allen walked to the batwing door and started to go out, but he stopped. He stepped back and to one side. He stood there watching something in the street for a moment. Then he walked back to where Comstock and the others were still sitting.

"That guy from the Snug T just rode into town with another cowhand," he said.

"What're they doing?" said Comstock, stiffening.

Allen shrugged. "I didn't stay to find out. I just come back here to tell you."

"Come on," said Comstock. "Let's see can we find out."

The whole bunch got up and went out on the sidewalk. "There they are down there at the general store," Allen said.

Comstock and the others looked. Chaney and his puncher had tied up in front of the store and were just going inside.

"Coming in from the Snug T Ranch," said Comstock, "they had to have been out there on that road."

"I bet it was them that shot at us," said Slab.

"Come on," said Comstock, and he led his four deputies across the street and down to the store. They went inside and found Chaney gathering up his goods. Chaney looked up to see them as they came in. "Howdy, Chaney," Comstock said. Chaney nodded. Comstock walked over to stand in front of him. The four deputies held back a ways, ready to draw their six-guns at the first sign of trouble. Chaney looked up at the fat sheriff.

"Something on your mind, Comstock?" he said.

Chaney's puncher moved back against the wall, watching the four deputies.

"Come into town for supplies, did you?" Comstock said.

"You can see that for yourself."

"You see or hear anything unusual out on the road on your way in here?"

"I don't recall anything," said Chaney.

"That's funny," said Comstock. "There was a bunch of shooting out there. Had to be just ahead of you, judging from the time you rode in."

"Were you involved in it?"

"Never mind that," Comstock said. "I'm just trying to figure how could you have come in when you did and not hear anything out there."

"Al," said the puncher, "we heard some shooting. Don't you remember? I said it sounded like maybe someone was shooting at coyotes somewheres up ahead of us."

"Oh, yeah," said Chaney. "I recall it now. It didn't seem too important, so I reckon I just kind of forgot about it. Was someone in some kind of trouble, Sheriff? Maybe we should have hurried on ahead to see if we could help out." He shook his head slowly. "Damn. We just thought it was someone shooting coyotes."

"You sure you didn't ride on up ahead and lend a hand?"

Chaney shook his head again. "We ain't had no trouble with coyotes lately at the Snug T," he said.

Comstock turned abruptly and headed for the front door. "Come on, boys," he said. The four deputies followed him out. When they had walked a few feet away from the store, Slab said, "Mr. Comstock, it was them two. You know it was."

"I know," Comstock.

"You going to just let them go?"

"It ain't time to fuck with them," Comstock said.

Back inside the store, Chaney looked over at his puncher. "Shooting coyotes," he said.

"Well," said the puncher, "they was."

# 17

Slocum rode out to check Molly's back fence. Her property in between the two fences was well enclosed by the steep valley walls. He had already repaired the fence that was close to the house, but Molly told him that it had been some time since the back fence had even been checked. The grass wasn't as green back there, and there was no water, so the cattle did not often get too close to it, but you never knew. They might. He found the fence and started riding it from the end nearest the valley wall to his right. He rode slowly, giving the fence a good looking over. He stopped at a couple of fence posts to tack up loose wire, but he found no breaks in the wire. It was mostly in good shape. By the time he was done, about half of the day had gone by. He turned to ride back to the house. Molly would have lunch ready by the time he got there.

Comstock's gang was still in his mind, but he had pushed them back somewhat. He was just about relaxed there with Molly. He had already spent some time with her, helping her with ranch chores, taking care of jobs that had been a bit too much for her to take care of, keeping track of her small herd of cattle. He was enjoying himself. And he did not expect to see Comstock or any of his men out this far away from Hangout. Molly told him that she had never been visited out there, not by anyone. He was beginning to feel a little bit guilty about having ignored the Comstock problem now for so long, but he eased his conscience a little by saying that the longer he stayed away, the more offguard he would catch them when he did decide to make his move. They probably, he thought, had already decided that he had simply skipped the county. It would make sense. He should have. But he couldn't. He kept thinking about the brutal way they had murdered poor old Tyson. He had to avenge that. Tyson had been a nice man. He had been harmless, and there was no excuse in the world for his killing.

Comstock and his four deputies had been out riding the range again. At a few of the small ranches, they had collected their taxes. At a few more, they had warned people that they would have to vacate in one week. Comstock had been keeping a meticulous list of the people who had been warned. He would go back in one week and drive them off. P.J. Merchand's name had a star drawn beside it on the list. After their last experience at Merchand's place, neither Comstock nor any of the four remaining deputies was anxious to go back. Comstock told himself that they would, but there was no hurry. He could be the last one, even after they had taken care of the Snug T.

The gang was out farther than they had gone yet. Comstock checked his list. He had one last place he wanted to hit on this day. It was a small ranch way out north of Hangout, the last place before the county line. It was owned by a man named Carl Morrison, who lived there along with his wife. They had no children and no ranch hands as far as Comstock knew. Comstock and his deputies were winding their way through the valleys, between the high hills. They had no desire to get caught trying to climb the steep walls again. Spike Allen was a stranger to this country, but he suddenly felt like he was in familiar territory.

"Say," he said, "ain't this that country where we chased Slocum?"

"Yeah," said Comstock. "We was up on top of that hill

right over yonder. He disappeared on us down in here some-wheres."

"We better keep our eyeballs peeled," said Slab. "He might could still be out here."

"It's possible," Comstock said. "I still think he's left these parts, but you can't never tell. I don't think we'll see him though. Ain't nothing for a man like him out here. Like I said, the only thing out here is the Morrison spread. A man and his wife. They couldn't afford to put him up for as long as he's been out. Couldn't afford to hire him on. He's either hiding out back at the Snug T or else he's left these parts."

"Just the same," said Slab, "I mean to keep a close watch."

They came across a winding stream and followed it across the valley floor and around a bend, and then they saw the Morrison ranch. "There it is, boys," said Comstock. They rode on up to the small house.

"Hell," said Slab, "these folks ain't going to have no money."

"Then they'll have one week," said Comstock, "and we'll have us one more ranch."

Before any of them could dismount, the door opened and Molly Morrison stepped into it holding a cocked shotgun in her hands.

"What do you want here?" she said.

"That ain't a very friendly greeting," said Comstock.

"What do you want?"

"Is your husband at home?"

Molly knew better than to tell them the truth. A woman alone in this country was always vulnerable to any band of ruffians. She saw the badges on the men's chests, but she also knew about Comstock and his gang.

"Not just now," she said, "but he's not far. He'll be com-ing back around real soon."

"You Miz Morrison?" Comstock said.

"That's right."

"Well, I reckon we can do business with you. I'm Sheriff Comstock, and we're riding out and around to collect on all the back taxes that folks owes to the county. I've got it down here that you all owes the county one hundred dollars. If you'll just pay up, we'll be on our way."

"We don't have a hundred dollars," Molly said, "and this is the first I've ever heard of taxes on this land anyhow."

"You can't pay?"

"No. And if I could, I don't think I would."

"Now, I'm sorry to hear that, ma'am," said Comstock. "If you're taxes ain't paid today, you'll have to vacate. I'm sorry about that, but it's the law. I'll give you one week to be off this place. A week from today, we'll be back to check."

As the sheriff was turning his horse to ride away, Molly said, "We'll still be here. You'd best come ready for a fight." Comstock's horse was turning around, when Comstock saw the rider coming. At first he thought that it might be Morrison. He thought he'd just keep going. After all, he had given the message to the missus. He didn't need to talk to her old man. But something about the size and shape of the horse made him hesitate. So far he could see the horse and rider only as a silhouette. He waited, and the other riders turned facing the same direction.

"Who is it?" said Slab. "Is it her husband?"

"I don't think so," said Comstock.

Molly grew nervous. She knew it was Slocum coming back. There was no one else out in that direction. She thought about firing a shot to warn him, but the gang might have turned on her and filled her full of holes. She waited, standing in the doorway with her shotgun. Slocum rode closer. He had not yet noticed the five men on horseback just in front of the ranch house. Suddenly Comstock recognized him though.

"It's Slocum," he said. "Shoot the son of a bitch."

Molly could not quite bring herself to shoot anyone in the back, so she fired her shotgun into the air over their heads, then stepped back and slammed her door, dropping the latch into place. The horses outside jumped, and Art Bacon was toppled from the saddle.

"God damn," he said, scrambling to his feet and reaching

for the reins to his loose horse. The others managed to control their mounts, but it took them a while to do that and then to get their guns out. Slocum had turned his big Appaloosa around and was hurrying back in the direction he had come from. Comstock and his crew started to ride after him.

"A thousand dollars," shouted Slab.

When they reached the near fence, they had to slow down and ride up the side of the hill far enough to go around the fence, then back down on the other side. Then they rode hard again, but Slocum was already out of sight. They continued after him anyway, hoping to catch up, straining their eyes for a glimpse of their prey and thinking about the money he was worth to them. Hack McGuire had the fastest horse of the bunch, and he was soon well out front. He rounded a bend in the side of the hill, and up ahead he saw Slocum. Slocum had turned his horse and was headed up the hillside. McGuire's heart raced with excitement. He would have the first chance at the money. He kept riding.

Slocum saw McGuire, too, but he was in no position to take a shot. Even if he had been, the distance would have been too great. He dismounted about halfway up the hill, pulling out his Winchester as he did. As his feet hit the ground, he slapped the Appaloosa on the rump. "Keep going, old boy," he said. "Go on." The big stallion kept moving toward the top of the hill, while Slocum looked around for some decent cover. There did not seem to be any nearby, and the rider down below was getting closer. He stood up straight and raised his rifle to his shoulder, taking aim at the deputy, who was still riding hard and fast. Just as he snapped off a shot, his foot slipped on loose rock. Slocum fell hard on his ass, and his shot went wide of the mark.

It did startle the deputy's horse though. McGuire was down and rolling with no rifle in his hands. Slocum started climbing. The rest of the sheriff's gang showed up where McGuire was standing, and the disappointed deputy pointed up the hill.

"There he goes," he told them.

Comstock and the deputies all dismounted and hauled out their rifles. Comstock laid his rifle across his saddle and tried to get a bead on Slocum, but he could not get his horse to stand still. Slab dropped to one knee and took aim, but his shot landed behind Slocum. Bacon and Allen fired rapid shots that went all over the place. Both shooters were standing. McGuire was chasing his horse so he could get his own rifle. Slocum reached the top of the hill and disappeared over the side.

Slab was the first one to remount. "Let's go get him," he shouted.

"Hold on, you damn fool," said Comstock.

"What's wrong?" Slab said.

"What do you think Slocum's up to?" Comstock said.

"He's running," said Slab, "and he's going to get away."

"He's got away," said Comstock, "and he ain't running no more. He's laid up there right now waiting for us to make a damn fool move like riding up that hillside after him. He could pick us off real easy one at a time. You still want to ride up there first? Go on if you do, but I'll stay down here and watch."

Slab rode toward the hillside. He stopped, hesitant, looking up toward the top. Slocum was nowhere to be seen. He turned his horse around and moved back a few feet, then turned around again.

"Aw, shit," he said. "Well, what the hell're we going to do?"

"We're just going to head back to Hangout and count our blessings," Comstock said.

Back at the ranch house, as soon as the sheriff and his gang had gone after Slocum, Molly had reloaded her shotgun, then changed her mind and taken up a six-gun. She hurried out the back door of the house and ran to the far hillside, where she took cover behind a clump of brush which grew just beside a large boulder. She hunkered down there to wait. It seemed like a long time just waiting there like that, but even-

tually the sheriff and deputies came riding back. She watched
as they rode toward her house.

"Let's stop here and question that gal again," Comstock said.
"She must know something about that son of a bitch."

He dismounted at her front door and called her name
while pounding on the door. When he received no answer,
he tried to open the door, but it wouldn't budge. It was bolted
from the inside. "Slab," he said, "go around and check the
back door." Slab rode his horse around the house and found
the door. He got off his horse and tried it. It opened. Taking
out his six-gun, he walked cautiously into the house. The
light was dim, but his eyes adjusted quickly. He walked
through the small house, then went to the front door and
tossed the board latch aside. He pushed open the door and
stepped out beside Comstock.

"She ain't in here," he said.

"Then she went out the back," said the sheriff. He started
riding around the house, followed by the others. Slab walked
back through to get the horse he had left at the back door.
Comstock and the others sat on prancing horses looking all
around, studying the hillside back there.

"Hell," said Comstock. "She could be anywhere. Let's get
on back to town."

Slocum watched from the top of the hill until Comstock and
the deputies were out of sight. Then he rounded up his Appaloosa and rode it along the hillside. He caught sight of
them again as they approached Molly's house, then watched
as they looked in and around the house. He saw them ride
away on their way back to Hangout. He had not heard any
more shots, so he thought that Molly was safe enough, but
he couldn't be sure. There were knives and ropes, and there
were hands of evil men that could strangle. He hurried down
the hillside as fast as he could safely go, then rode hard to
the fence, up and around the fence slowly, then hard again
to the ranch house. He pulled up close to the house and
stepped inside.

"Molly," he called out. There was no answer. He ran quickly through the house, checking as he went, and then he went out the back door. "Molly," he called again. This time Molly stepped out of her hiding place.

"I'm here, Slocum," she yelled. She ran toward him. When she reached him, she threw her arms around him and squeezed him tight. Then she stepped back.

"Thank God you're safe," he said.

"You, too," she said.

"What happened back here?"

"They came up to the house and demanded a hundred dollars for back taxes," Molly said. "When I didn't cough it right up, they gave me one week to clear out. They were about to leave when they spotted you riding back. You know the rest."

"Well, most of it anyway. I guess that was your shot that warned me?"

"Yeah. I fired it off, then slammed the door and latched it and went out the back."

"That was smart of you," he said. "And I thank you for the warning."

"Any time," she said. "Say, I've got food and coffee inside. You ready for it?"

"I'm more than ready."

They went into the house and sat down to eat. When they were done, Molly poured Slocum another cup of coffee. He leaned back and took a sip.

"Molly," he said.

"What?"

"I've been laying around up here too long. Comstock surprised me today by coming this far out. No telling what he's been up to closer in to Hangout. I've got to go back and finish this thing."

She sighed heavily. "Well," she said, "I knew it was coming."

"I want you to go with me back to the Snug T," he said. "You'll be safe there till it's all over."

"I can take care of myself right here," she said. "There's work to be done, and—"

"The work can wait. Your cows have good water and good grazing. I don't want to be worrying about Comstock and them coming back out here and catching you alone. If you don't agree to ride back with me, I'll just have to throw you across a saddle and take you."

"Since you put it that way," she said, "I guess I'll go voluntarily."

# 18

P.J. Merchand was prying at a stump to the side of his house with a long bar, trying to root it out. Tex, the cowhand Chaney had sent over to stay with Merchand, was watching the road. He looked back and saw Merchand struggling with the stump, and he walked over. "Let me give you a hand here," he said.

"Al didn't send you over here to work," said Merchand.

"Hell, that's all right. I can help you out a bit," Tex said. He backed up to the stump and squatted down, getting a grip on the thing with both hands. "Let's go," he said. While Tex strained, lifting with his legs, Merchand started prying with the long bar again. At last, creaking and popping, the stump broke loose. Tex fell over, and Merchand lost his balance, but shuffling quickly, he caught his footing and stayed on his feet.

"God damn," he said. He tossed the bar down and stuck out a hand to help Tex get up. "By God," he said, "we done it."

Standing up and dusting off his britches, Tex grinned. "It ain't so hard when you got two a-working at it," he said.

Out on the road Comstock and his gang were just returning to Hangout from their latest trip out in the county to do meanness. Slab hauled back on his reins and pointed. Comstock stopped his horse to look, and the others stopped behind them. Slab was pointing at Merchand and Tex out in the yard. Apparently they had not noticed the sheriff's gang. Slab hauled out his rifle and looked at Comstock.

"Shall I?" he said.

"Go ahead," said the sheriff.

Slab cranked a shell into the chamber, raised the rifle to his shoulder and took aim. At the same time, Art Bacon pulled out his rifle and did the same. Slab squeezed the trigger. A second later, Bacon fired his weapon. Slab's shot caught Merchand square in the back, and almost immediately, Bacon's shot crashed into Tex's sternum. Merchand fell sprawling across the recently uprooted stump, and Tex was thrown back, landing in the dirt, staring upward with blank eyes.

"Good work, boys," said Comstock. "Let's get to town."

"You don't want to check and make sure they're dead?" said Spike Allen.

"They're dead enough," said Comstock. "Come on."

It was a little later when Slocum and Molly came riding down the same road on their way to the Snug T. They had arrived at about the same spot in the road where Comstock's men had fired their deadly shots. Molly was the one who noticed the bodies lying beside the house. "Slocum," she said. "Look over there." Slocum looked over and saw what she had seen.

"Let's take a closer look," he said. They rode over to the house and saw what had happened. "This is Comstock's work all right," Slocum said. "They were ambushed. Never had a chance." He dismounted and went looking for a shovel. The burying finished, he and Molly mounted their horses and continued the ride toward the Snug T. When they got close to Hangout, Slocum led the way around town to avoid being seen. He wanted an encounter with Comstock and his gang, but not with Molly around. By the time they arrived at the Snug T, it was well past noon. They rode straight up to the ranch house and dismounted. Slocum walked up on the porch and knocked on the door. There was no answer. He went back to his horse.

"No one seems to be around," he said.

"What do we do?" said Molly.

"I guess we ride out and look for someone."

He was about to swing back up into the saddle when a cowhand came walking around from behind the house. "Hey, Slocum," the puncher said, "what brings you back?"

"Howdy," Slocum said. "Where's the boss?"

"If you mean Miss Pearlie, she's gone with Charlie Bob and Flank Steak to the capital. If you mean Al, you oughta find him over around the corral."

"Thanks, Ben," Slocum said. He remounted and led Molly to the corral. Chaney came walking out of the tack room just then and saw him.

"Slocum," he said. "I'm glad to see you. Hell, we didn't know if you were still around these parts."

"I still got a job to do," Slocum said. "Al, do you know Molly Morrison?"

Chaney stepped up closer and extended a hand to Molly. "No," he said, "but I'm pleased to meet you, ma'am."

"This is Al Chaney," Slocum said. "He's the foreman here."

"I'm glad to know you, Mr. Chaney," said Molly.

"Just call me Al," he said. "I never even heard my daddy called Mr. Chaney."

"Molly's got a little spread up near the county line," said Slocum. "Comstock just paid her a visit. He gave her a week to clear out. I convinced her she'd be safer here till this whole business is finished."

"Good idea, Slocum. There's plenty of room in the house, and Pearlie won't mind a bit. Comstock's been doing a lot of that lately. He told ole P.J. Merchand the same thing. I sent Tex over to stay with him."

"We just came by there," Slocum said. "We found both of them shot dead."

"Oh no," said Chaney. "Damn it. I told P.J. to come over

here, but he wouldn't have anything to do with the idea. The stubborn old fool."

Molly glanced at Slocum. "I guess I'm glad that you made me listen," she said.

"Well, let's go over to the house," said Chaney, "and I'll get you settled in."

Chaney was on foot, so Slocum and Molly walked along with him, leading their horses. "Al," said Slocum.

"Yeah?"

"We got to stop Comstock before he does any more murders."

"You got an idea?" said Chaney.

"First off, I'd say send out some boys and round up all the rest of the small ranchers. Bring them over here. We can't keep our eyes on all the ranches, but if we don't do something, he's liable to kill them all."

"Some of them are pretty stubborn," said Chaney, "like P.J. was."

"Then tell them what happened to P.J."

"We'll do our damndest," said Chaney. "What else?"

"Comstock's gang has been whittled down to four," Slocum said. "He's outnumbered. I don't mean for the Snug T to get involved in an open war with him, but he don't know that. I expect him to be out recruiting some more gunhands sometime real soon. I don't expect he'll ride out for them with just four men, but he might. I'll be watching the road to the capital. He might send a wire."

"You think we'd ought to cut the wire?"

"I'm thinking about it," Slocum said.

In Hangout, Comstock stepped out of the telegraph office with a satisfied expression on his face. Slab and the rest of the boys were on the sidewalk waiting. Slab gave the sheriff an inquiring look.

"I sent it," Comstock said. "I made it sound desperate as hell, too. The governor will most likely be sending us a small army."

"Do we need to wait for his answer?" said Slab.

"Naw," said Comstock. "Ole Chormley will bring it to me down to the Bird's Beak. Let's go."

They started walking toward the saloon. Along the way, Slab was thinking. His face was all wrinkled up. "Mr. Comstock," he said.

"What is it?"

"I been wondering. If the governor picks out some deputies to send down here to help us out, they're liable to be a bunch of straight shooters. You know?"

"I'm the sheriff," said Comstock, "and you boys are my deputies. Just remember that. While the governor's men are here to help us out, we'll all just play everything as straight as they do. That's all. Once they've helped us wipe out Slocum and the Snug T bunch, why, I'll thank them and send them on back to the capital, and we'll resume our normal activities. Understand?"

"Yeah. Yeah. I guess I kind of forget now and then that we're really the law in these parts."

They reached the Bird's Beak Saloon and turned in through the batwing doors, heading for their regular table. Comstock waved at Lonnie, the barkeep, as he passed by. Lonnie got a bottle and five glasses and hustled on over to the table. "Where's the boss?" said Comstock.

"He's back in his office, Sheriff," the barkeep said.

"Business been good?"

"Never better."

"Thanks, Lonnie."

The bartender turned to walk back to the bar. Comstock downed his first drink and stood up. "Come with me, Slab," he said. Slab turned his down and followed the sheriff, who walked over to the office door, rapped once, opened it and stepped in. The man behind the desk looked up surprised.

"Comstock," he said. "How can I help you?"

He was a tall, thin man wearing most of a three-piece suit. The black jacket was hanging on a peg on the wall beside a black gambler's hat. A string tie adorned the man's throat, and a pencil-thin mustache looked almost as if it had been drawn over his upper lip.

"I understand your business has been doing pretty well, Snapper," Comstock said.

"Well," said Snapper, "I can't complain."

Comstock reached under his vest and pulled out a piece of paper which he unfolded and appeared to read. "According to my records," he said, "you owe a thousand dollars in back taxes. You want to be paying that now?"

Snapper looked astonished. He glanced from Comstock to the evil-looking Slab.

"I thought the taxes you've been collecting have just been on ranch property," he said.

"It's all property in the county," said Comstock.

"No one ever said anything to me about it before."

"I'm saying it now. You going to pay?"

"What if I don't?"

"You lose the place. You get one week to clear out."

Snapper stood up and walked to a large floor safe. He looked back at Comstock and the deputy. "If you'll excuse me," he said, "I'll get it and bring it out to you."

"That's all right," the sheriff said. "Just go right on ahead. We don't mind waiting."

Snapper got down on one knee in an attempt to hide his actions from his two unwelcome visitors. In a minute, he had the safe open, and he reached for a stack of bills. He closed the safe as quickly as he could, then stood up, turned and faced Comstock. He held out the bundle. Comstock took it and tucked it in a pocket.

"Don't I get a receipt or something?" said Snapper.

"I trust you," said Comstock. "Why don't you trust me?"

He turned and walked out of the office. Slab slowly backed out the door, smiling at Snapper all the way. When he got out, he pulled the door shut and returned to the table. Comstock took out the thousand and counted out five equal shares. He pocketed one and shoved the others around the table. The deputies could hardly believe their eyes. To a man, they would have attacked the U.S. capital for their leader.

●    ●    ●

Out on the road, Slocum climbed a pole and cut the telegraph wires. He went back down and mounted his Appaloosa. Then he moved a little farther down the road to a good place from which to hide and watch. If he could help it, Comstock would not get any more help. He wanted to wait for Pearlie and the two cowboys to get back to the Snug T before he made any kind of outright assault on Comstock and the other four. He wanted to be sure that once the sheriff and his cronies were wiped out, there would be no one to blame for it but Slocum. He would be the only fugitive from justice to come out of this battle, and when it was over, he would ride hard and fast for some place like northern California or Oregon or Washington. Hell, he might even have to go to Canada. They wouldn't be able to touch him up there, and at least they talked English up there. It wouldn't be like going to Mexico. But then, he just remembered, he had heard that there was one place up there where everyone talked French. He'd have to be careful to avoid that place. He did not know a single goddamned word of French.

A small, neatly dressed man approached the governor in his smoking room in the mansion. It was late. "I'm sorry, sir," the man said. "Ordinarily I wouldn't have bothered you, but this telegram came in late. I thought it might be something you'd want to see."

The governor held out a hand for it. "Thank you," he said. Then man handed the telegram to the governor and stepped back a polite distance to wait. The governor read over the message and looked up.

"He wants more deputies," he said. "The situation is getting out of hand. Find Marshal Brandon, Edgar, and send him to me at once."

"Yes, sir."

The little man called Edgar disappeared, and the governor picked up the telegram again and studied it as if he might learn more from it on a second reading. He did not, of course. He stood up and walked over to a side table, where he found a good cigar. He picked up a tool and nipped off the end.

Then he struck a match and lit the cigar. He poured himself a snifter of brandy, and with the brandy and the cigar, he went back to his easy chair and sat down. He did not have long to wait. There was a light rap on the door.

"Yes?" he called out.

The door opened slightly, and Edgar stuck his head in. "I have Marshal Brandon, Governor," he said.

"Send him in."

"Yes, sir."

Edgar moved aside, opening the door wide. Marshal Brandon stepped in, and Edgar pulled the door shut from the outside, leaving the governor and the marshal alone.

"Sit down, Cy," the governor said.

The marshal took a chair.

"Can I offer you a cigar? A brandy?"

"No, thanks, sir."

"Cy, how many good deputies can you scrape up in a hurry?"

"I could come up with about six without hurting the situation here."

"Gather them up as quickly as you can. I want you to ride with them down to Hangout. There's a bad situation there, and they need our help. Before you leave, I'll give you the names of the parties on both sides of the conflict. I'll give you some details that I think you'll need, and I'll give you the name of a contact. I want you to be ready to move out first thing in the morning."

# 19

There were only five men left to deal with. Slocum had faced worse odds. He was ready for a bloodbath, but he did not want it to take place in town, where innocent people might be hurt or killed. He was watching the road to the capital most of the time, hoping that Comstock or any or all of his deputies might try to make a run for that place. So far he had not seen any of them. He kept watching though. They might try for the capital or they might ride out to some of the smaller ranches again. They had given Molly one week. Likely they had seen others that same day, and they would have to ride out to attempt to take over the ranches when the week was up. Either way, Slocum wanted to be ready to catch them out of town. He could easily pick off two or three of them from his hiding place. Those that remained shouldn't be too much of a problem.

Pearlie and her two escorts were nearing Hangout. They were returning by the main road. Pearlie did not anticipate any trouble riding back through Hangout to the Snug T. Comstock and his gang had only been trying to prevent her from riding to the capital. They might be pissed off if they saw her returning, but she did not think they would try anything. She and the two hands had stopped along the way at a stream that ran by the road, to rest the horses, let them graze and

149

water. Pearlie sat down leaning her back against a tree. Flank
Steak took the makings out of his pocket and rolled a cigarette and lit it. Charlie Bob was pacing near the road.

"We're almost back, boys," said Pearlie.

"Yes, ma'am," said Flank Steak. "What'll be our next
move?"

"I don't know exactly," she said. "We'll go straight back
to the ranch and let Al know what's happened. Then I hope
there's some way to get the word out to Slocum. I wish I
knew where he was hanging out."

"Well," said Charlie Bob, "me and Flank Steak could ride
out and try to hunt him down."

"We just may have to do that," she said.

"In the meantime," said Flank Steak, "are we just going
to ride right smack through Hangout and hope for the best?"

"I been thinking about that," said Pearlie. "I don't think
Comstock will mess with us, but I can't be sure of that. It
might be best if we were to swing off the road here and ride
wide around the town."

"Yes, ma'am," said Flank Steak.

"It won't add more than an hour, hour and a half, to our
ride," said Charlie Bob.

"Well, let's do it then," said Pearlie. She stood up and
stretched. "You boys about ready to hit it again?"

"Yes, ma'am," said Flank Steak.

"Let's ride," said Charlie Bob.

They mounted up and headed off the main road in order
to swing around Hangout. Slocum was hidden off the side
of the road just about a half mile on down, waiting for some
sign of Comstock and his gang.

Back at the capital, Marshal Brandon had gathered up six of
the best deputy marshals he could find. They were all sea-
soned veterans, good men in a fight. He knew each man well,
called each a friend, had ridden with each of them and fought
with them before on numerous occasions. He felt good about
his posse. It was early in the morning when they gathered.
Each man had a good horse, a revolver and a rifle, and plenty

of ammunition. They had a chuck wagon and cook riding along with them. They were set for as long as this job would take. Brandon took note that the governor was in his office early that morning, so he stopped by on his way out to receive any final instructions the governor might have for them. It didn't take long, and soon they were on their way. They made a formidable-looking unit as they moved onto the road.

Sheriff Comstock had gathered his four deputies together in his office. It was not too early, for none of them liked rising early in the morning. They were usually sitting up late drinking, so they needed time to sleep it off. They all felt pretty good. Comstock had kept them in pocket money from the beginning. Their only problem was that damned Slocum. As soon as they took care of him, they would have clear sailing.

"Boys," said Comstock, "I've got some business to take care of here in town today, but I've done rode out with you to all the ranches, so you ought to be able to find your way around."

"Don't worry about that, Mr. Comstock," said Slab. "I've got all the roads and trails set firm in my mind."

"Good. What I want you to do is to get around to as many of the ranches as you can today. Kick all the bastards out. They had their chance to pay up, and they didn't do it. If they resist, kill them. They'll be resisting the law." He picked up a piece of paper from the top of his desk and handed it to Slab. "Here's the list of who paid and who didn't. You can get started right away."

"What about Slocum?" said Art Bacon.

"If you run across him," said Comstock, "kill him. Otherwise don't worry about him. The governor's men ought to be showing up any day now. We'll have a better chance with more men."

Slab was studying the list Comstock had given him. "I don't see the Snug T on here," he said.

"Leave them alone till the new deputies get here," said the sheriff. "We don't need to be taking no chances."

"All right," said Slab. "Let's go."

He studied the list again once he and the others were all mounted up. Then he led his bunch, not down the main road, but off in another direction which he fancied was a shortcut to one of the ranches. When they made it out to the ranch, they found it abandoned.

"I guess we scared him off all right," said Hack McGuire.

"He don't seem to have packed up anything," said Slab. "It looks like he just lit out."

He put a check mark beside the name on the list. Then he tucked the pencil and paper back into his pocket. "Let's get on to the next one," he said.

They found the second ranch in the same condition as the first one. The third one was also abandoned, with all its tools and its animals still there. They checked inside the house and found everything in place.

"This here is pretty weird, Slab," said Spike Allen.

"Well, hell," said Slab, "we told them to pay up or to get out within a week. They didn't pay and they've got out. I guess we was pretty convincing all right."

Art Bacon laughed. "Yeah," he said. "We're a mean-looking bunch of son of a bitches."

Slocum grew tired of watching the road. He was tired, too, of his own cooking. He wanted a good hot meal, and he wanted a drink of good brown whiskey. He had waited out the morning and into the afternoon. He decided to abandon the post and take a ride into town. It was likely a foolish move, but his mood was reckless. He found his big Appaloosa and put the saddle back on. He shoved the Winchester into the boot and mounted up. It was a short ride into Hangout from the place he had posted himself. As he rode into the town, he rode slowly, looking on both sides of the street. He did not really want to get into a gunfight in town, but he would be ready for anything. As he moved past the businesses, he saw no sign of the sheriff or any of his deputies. He stopped in front of a little eatery. Dismounting, he tied his horse to the hitch rail and went inside.

There weren't many customers in the place for it was well

past lunchtime. Slocum took a seat at a table where he could face the door. In less than a minute, a man in a greasy apron came over.

"I got steak and I got ham," the man said.

"Bring me steak," said Slocum. "What you got to go with it?"

" 'Taters and bread," the man said. "Beans."

"Bring them all, and a cup of coffee while I'm waiting."

The man went away. Slocum looked over the few customers in the place. He did not recognize any of them. The man came back with the coffee. It was stale, but Slocum drank it anyhow. By the time he had finished it, the man brought his meal. It wasn't the best Slocum had ever had, but he ate it. The coffee he had been served must have been the end of the pot, for when the man came back and poured him a refill, it was much better. He had two more cups. He paid the man and walked out onto the sidewalk. He stood there for a moment studying the street. Still he recognized no one. It was a little early in the day, but he decided he would venture into the Bird's Beak for a drink. He was feeling bold and more than a little belligerent.

Comstock was inside the Bird's Beak. He had just finished a drink and was about to walk back to his office. He really wasn't busy at all. He had just told his deputies that because he had not wanted to ride with them. He was worried about running into Slocum out there somewhere. He reached the batwing doors and was about to step onto the sidewalk when he spotted Slocum across the street mounting his big Appaloosa.

"Damn," he said, not quite under his breath. He stood there watching. Slocum rode across the street and dismounted again, tying the horse to the rail outside the saloon. Comstock hurried back to his table. He was alone. He had sent all his deputies out. What a fool he had been. He sure as hell did not want to fight Slocum by himself. And Slocum was already wanted for murder. He wouldn't likely hesitate to shoot down a sheriff, even in front of witnesses. Comstock considered going to the bar and asking the barkeep for the loan of his shotgun. Then he could blast Slocum as he came through the door. He glanced over at the bar and saw Snapper there in conversation with the bartender. Snapper would not let him use the scattergun. He would much rather see him shot down. He couldn't think of anything else to do, so he hurried back to his table at the far end of the place and sat down. Just as he did, Slocum walked through the door.

Slocum hesitated at the door and looked around the room. He spotted Comstock right off, and he also noticed that the man was alone. The deputies might be down at the office, or they might be out on Comstock's dirty business. Slocum had no way of knowing. He did not let on that he had seen Comstock. He walked straight over to the bar and ordered a shot of whiskey. Looking into the big mirror behind the bar, he could see the sheriff. He could tell that Comstock was nervous. Well, the son of a bitch had every reason to be. Slocum sipped his whiskey and tried to decide what to do.

He could easily kill Comstock. He knew it. But he had told himself that he did not want to get into a shooting match in town. If he were to shoot the crooked sheriff, the deputies might come running to see what was going on. Then folks would be in danger. He decided against shooting. He sipped at the whiskey again. He watched as Comstock poured himself another glass and drank it down in gulps. That's good, he said to himself. Let him get drunk as a skunk. He took another sip and finished his drink. Then he called for another. He picked that one up in his left hand and turned to look directly at Comstock. He started walking toward the sheriff. Comstock stiffened.

"You want some company," Slocum said, "or do you like to drink alone?"

"What are you doing in town?" Comstock said. "You're a wanted man."

"It's nice to be wanted," Slocum said, pulling out a chair and setting his drink on the table. He sat down directly across from the sheriff. Comstock's right hand dropped beneath the table.

"I'd keep my hands in sight," said Slocum. "I've killed men for hiding their hands under the table."

The sheriff's hand came back up to rest on the tabletop.

"There's witnesses here," he said.

"Like you said, I'm already a wanted man. What do I care if I kill you in front of witnesses?"

"Some of these in here are law-abiding men. If you gun me down, they're liable to all start shooting at you. Besides, I've got a price on your head. They might just try for that."

Slocum picked up his drink and took a sip. "I haven't seen you for a while, Comstock," he said, "especially not without your gang around you."

"They ain't far away," Comstock lied. "I was you, I'd be getting out of here as fast as I could. I'd be getting far off. I'm surprised you ain't left the country."

"I've got something to do first," said Slocum. "I had a good friend here, a man named Tyson. He was murdered in cold blood by a slimey, chicken shit son of a bitch."

"Now wait a minute. I ain't—"

"I don't mean to leave these parts as long as that no-good cowardly bastard is still alive."

Slocum picked up his drink again, but this time he did not take a sip. Suddenly and with no warning, he tossed the contents across the table into Comstock's face. The whiskey burned the sheriff's eyes. His hands went up to his face. Slocum got to his feet and tossed the table to one side. He grabbed Comstock by his shirtfront, lifting him to his feet. Behind the bar, the bartender reached for the shotgun, but Snapper put a hand on his wrist stopping him.

"Let it go, Lonnie," he said.

Lonnie gave Snapper a curious look, but he put the shotgun down.

Still holding Comstock by his shirt, Slocum slapped him hard across the face three times. Then he reached down and pulled the sheriff's six-gun out of its holster and tossed it across the room. He drove a right deep into Comstock's paunchy gut, still holding the sheriff by his shirt with his left hand. Otherwise, the blow to the belly would have doubled the sorry wretch over. Comstock was gasping for breath. Slocum hit him hard in the mouth, cutting his lips. Blood ran from the sheriff's mouth. Slocum turned his shirt loose, letting Comstock fall to the floor on his hands and knees. Slocum reached down, pulled him back up to his feet and drove another right into the side of his head, closing an eye. Comstock fell back flat.

As Slocum walked toward him, the crooked lawman rolled over onto his belly. He struggled to get back up. As his knees were drawn up under him and his ass was sticking up in the air, Slocum delivered a swift kick to the rear, the toe of his boot lapping underneath to bust Comstock's balls. Comstock moaned pitifully.

"Comstock," said Slocum.

The sheriff groaned.

"Comstock, you sleazy son of a bitch. Do you hear me?"

"Yeah. I—Oh—I hear."

"The next time I see you, I'm going to do worse. You got that? I'm going to kick the shit out of you till you try to stop me with a bullet. You and all your damn deputies. Are you listening?"

The sheriff moaned again, and Slocum kicked him in the ribs.

"Are you listening?"

"Yes. Yes."

"I won't be far away, and I won't be hard to find."

Slocum turned and walked across the room and out through the batwings. In the street, he mounted his Appaloosa and turned to ride out of town.

# 20

As Slocum rode away from Hangout, he wondered whether or not he had done the right thing. He could have killed Comstock easily, but he had chosen not to. Instead he had simply beaten the man badly and humiliated him in front of a score or so townfolks. Riding along and musing, he decided that he had done good. The crooked sheriff did not deserve a quick and easy end. This way he would suffer longer. It served the son of a bitch right. The only thing that could possibly be wrong with it would be if one of the outlaw posse should get lucky and kill Slocum while Comstock was still alive. Well, he would just have to be damn careful and make sure that did not happen.

He had no real idea where he was going. He just wanted to get away from town for a spell. But he did not want to get too far away. He meant to watch for the posse and catch them their next time out. He spotted a clump of trees beside a creek only a few miles out, and he decided to camp there. It would be a pretty good joke. Should the Comstock bunch get after him, they would never look so close to town. He stopped at the trees and unsaddled the Appaloosa, allowing the horse to graze at his leisure. Then he set about making his small camp.

• • •

When the deputies returned to town, they did not find Comstock in the Bird's Beak. They just stepped inside and looked around. When they did not spot the sheriff, they turned and went back out. No one inside had a chance to say anything to them. Out on the sidewalk, Slab said, "Let's check at the office." They left their horses tied in front of the saloon and walked over to the sheriff's office. He was sitting behind his desk. Stepping inside, they immediately noticed Comstock's condition.

"What the hell happened to you?" Slab said.

"Never mind that," said Comstock. "Where the hell have you been?"

"We been riding the circuit," said Slab. "Just like you told us to. We found every ranch deserted. I figure we scared them all off."

"That's good," said Comstock. He patted his forehead with his pocket handkerchief. One eye was swollen shut, and there was blood caked on the side of his head. His suit was rumpled and dirty from rolling on the floor and tussling with Slocum. "He came into town while you were gone," he said.

"Who? Slocum?"

"Who else? God damn it. He must have been watching. He waited until you were all out of town and I was left in here by myself. He caught me in the saloon and beat the crap out of me. After I was down, he kicked me. The son of a bitch."

"Where is he now?"

"He rode out of town. He wanted to get out before you came back. He's a chicken shit is what he is."

Slab thought, I doubt that, but he kept his thought to himself. "You want us to go after him?" he asked.

"I want him dead," said the sheriff, "but, no. I don't want you going after him just now. He's well away from here by this time. Ain't no telling which way he went either. He could be anywhere out there."

"You don't s'pose he's gone back out to the Snug T, do you?" Slab said.

"I doubt it," said Comstock, "but you never know. He could be out there."

"We could go check the place over."

"Not yet," Comstock said. "I don't feel like riding just now. And I damn sure don't want you riding out and leaving me here again. I don't believe Slocum'll come back in today, but you can't tell. He might have found himself a spot somewheres where he can watch. If that's what he's doing, then if you ride out again, he might just ride right back in. He might just kill me the next time. No. Let's wait for the new deputies. They ought to be showing up just any day now. In the meantime, remember, if you spot the bastard, kill him. Shoot first. Don't give him a chance."

"Don't worry about that," said Slab. "If I lay eyes on him, he's a dead man."

Spike Allen spoke up next, saying, "Well, if we ain't going out now, what say we go on over to the Bird's Beak and have a drink or two?"

"Or more," said Hack McGuire.

Comstock was about to say no. The Bird's Beak was where he had been so recently humiliated. Some of the same people were likely to still be in there, and he didn't want them looking at him, grinning, maybe even laughing at him. The sons of bitches. God damn it, but he wanted to kill Slocum badly, not badly enough to take any chances, but he sure did want to kill him. He wondered if his deputies could wound the man and disarm him, then bring him around to Comstock to finish off. That would be ideal. He thought about telling them that and doubling the reward if they could accomplish it, but he did not. Instead it occurred to him that if he stayed away the men in the Bird's Beak would think that he was too embarrassed to show his face. He decided that he would not allow that. He pushed back his chair and stood up.

"Come on," he said. "Let's go get them drinks."

They walked back to the Bird's Beak and stalked inside like they owned the place. As they passed by the bar on the way to their usual table, each man grabbed himself a glass and Comstock called for a bottle. Lonnie put it on the bar, and Comstock grabbed it by the neck and followed his men on over to the table. Lonnie wrote down the bottle in a little book he kept behind the bar. At the table Comstock poured the first round. They had finished the first drink and poured a second when old Chormley from the telegraph office came running in. He hurried over to the table where Comstock was sitting and handed him a piece of paper.

"It's the answer to your telegraph," he said. "It just came in."

Comstock snatched it out of Chormley's hand and read it. He brushed Chormley away with his left hand, and the telegrapher turned and walked out. Comstock leaned back in his chair and grinned. He picked up his drink and gulped it down.

"The governor's sending a U.S. marshal and six deputies," he said. "We'll sit tight till they get here." He lifted the telegram and held it in front of his eyes, although he could only see out of one of them. "Yes sir," he said. "The governor says, 'U.S. marshal and six deputies on the way.' By God, we'll get them now."


Al Chaney was sitting alone on the front porch when the three ragged-looking riders came toward the house. He stood up, squinting until he could recognize them for sure. It was Pearlie, Flank Steak and Charlie Bob. Chaney jumped off the porch and ran toward them. He was about halfway when Pearlie saw him coming. She dismounted, and Flank Steak took the reins from her. She ran to meet Chaney. When they came together, they threw their arms around each other.

"Pearlie," Chaney said, "I'm glad you're back."

"Me, too," she said. "Let's get these horses taken care of, and then—"

"Me and Flank Steak will do that, ma'am," said Charlie Bob. "Howdy, Al."

"Charlie Bob," said Chaney. "Flank Steak. Glad to have you back. Thanks for watching out for Pearlie."

"It was our pleasure," said Charlie Bob.

"Part of the job," said Flank Steak.

The two cowboys headed for the corral, Charlie Bob leading Pearlie's horse. Chaney glanced at them as they rode. "Say," he said, "you got a new horse."

"Yeah," she said. "Mine broke a leg along the way. We had to shoot it."

As they reached the porch and started to mount the steps, Chaney said, "Did you see the governor?"

"Yeah," she said. "I saw him all right. Wait a minute though. Let me get something to drink."

"There's lemonade in the kitchen," Chaney said, "or would you like something stronger?"

Pearlie sank down in a chair on the porch. "Bring me a glass of that lemonade," she said, "and bring along a whiskey bottle."

Chaney went inside. In a couple of minutes he came back with two glasses, one filled with lemonade, and the whiskey bottle. He sat down and handed the lemonade to Pearlie. The glass was full, and she drank it down a little. Chaney had just poured whiskey into his glass, and Pearlie held out her lemonade. He poured whiskey in it. She took another drink and then leaned back in her chair with a heavy sigh.

"Well?" said Chaney.

"We saw the governor," she said. "Comstock had been there first. He'd told a passel of lies and asked for some more deputies. The governor authorized him to hire some on. He also told the governor that it was Slocum who killed Uncle Reggie. Well, I set him straight. Told him the whole story. Everything. He said he'd send a new batch of lawmen to clean things up. He said that everything we had done, including Slocum, was cleared. If we have any trouble with Comstock before the new lawmen get here, we can do what we have to do."

"He said all that?"

"He sure did. Now, where's Slocum?"

"I'm damned if I know. He hasn't been around except to bring in that gal Molly to stay here."

"Molly?" said Pearlie.

"She has a ranch way out by the county line. She was the first one. He had me to send the boys out and round up all the small ranchers. They're all here now. All except for poor ole Merchand. They killed him, and our man Tex with him."

"Well," said Pearlie, "it's just about over, I guess. It's hard to believe. There's just the one thing."

"What's that?"

"Slocum's out there somewhere by himself thinking that he's still a wanted man. We've got to let him know somehow."

"I'll send some boys out looking for him tomorrow," said Chaney.

"Be sure to tell them how important it is they find him and tell him," she said. "He has to know."

"Yeah, I will. First thing in the morning. Right now, darlin', let's go inside. You've had a long ride. You must be tired."

"I been thinking, Sheriff," said Slab, his words slurring slightly, "if we wait for them new deputies and that U.S. marshal before we go after Slocum, well, they might be straight arrows like we talked about before. They might just arrest him and take him in. Then me and the boys would lose our chance at that thousand-dollar reward you promised."

Comstock downed his drink and poured another.

"I reckon that's a possibility," he said. He thought about the pleasure he would get at the killing of Slocum. He also thought about the danger in the attempt. But he had never hated anyone as much as he hated Slocum.

"Couldn't we at least pay us a visit to the Snug T in the morning," Slab said, "and check around a bit and see if maybe he's hiding out there?"

Comstock sipped at his drink. "Well," he said, "we might could do that."

"We'd look better to them federal lawmen," said Art Bacon, "if we was to get the baddest of them all before they was to show up."

"That's right," said Slab. "The word would be bound to get back to the governor, too. It'd make a big man out of you."

Comstock did not like his deputies putting ideas into his head. He did not respond immediately. He sipped some more of his drink. Just then Snapper came out of his office, and Comstock saw him glance in his direction. Snapper went behind the bar and started talking in a low voice with Lonnie. Comstock thought that they were looking in his direction. They were talking about him, probably talking about the fight he'd had with Slocum in there earlier that day. Suddenly he hated Snapper almost as much as he hated Slocum. He thought that he would like to kill everyone who had witnessed his beating, Snapper most of all.

"We'd be outnumbered out there," he said.

"You think they'd start trouble?"

Comstock sipped again. "I don't think so. I don't think they would. We'd just be looking around for Slocum," he said. "That's all."

He tried to figure out what had happened. Who had turned the conversation around? It was now as if he were the one arguing for the trip out to the Snug T in the morning and Slab was the one questioning its wisdom. Had Slab done that to him? He wasn't sure, but now he could go on and approve the ride without it seeming as if Slab was the one with the idea. He downed the rest of his drink and stood up.

"Boys," he said, "I think we'll all ride out to the Snug T in the morning. They might could be harboring a fugitive out there. We need to have a talk with them and look around the place. I want you all to be ready to ride first thing in the morning. We'll meet over at the office."

He had spoken loud so that everyone in the place could hear him. Then he turned to walk toward the door. As he passed by the bar, Snapper stopped him

"Sheriff," he said.

Comstock turned to face Snapper.

"What can I do for you?" he asked.

"I'd like it if you was to pay your bar bill," said Snapper.

"You'll get paid."

"I'd like to get paid now."

"I said you'll get your damned money," said the sheriff.

"I paid your taxes when you told me to," Snapper said. "I don't believe they were really authorized. I think you made them up. But I paid them. Now I want your bar bill paid."

"We'll talk about it later," said Comstock, and he turned back toward the door. Snapper reached under the bar and brought out the shotgun, slamming it down on the bar.

"Now," he said. He pulled back the hammer. Everyone in the bar grew silent. All eyes were on Snapper and Comstock. A few men who were seated behind Comstock, fearful of being in the line of stray buckshot, got up and moved to the sides. Comstock stared at Snapper for a moment with hatred in his one good eye. Suddenly his expression relaxed and he smiled.

"Okay, Snapper," he said. "Why not?" He reached into a pocket and pulled out a wad of bills as he walked closer to the bar. He slapped some of the bills on the bar. Snapper looked at him for a bit. This was too easy. At last, he turned loose of the shotgun and reached for the money. As he did so, Comstock pulled out his six-gun and fired. The bullet smashed into Snapper's sternum and splattered blood on the shelves and glasses and mirror behind the bar. Snapper's face registered surprise, astonishment. He stood for a moment rocking. His knees buckled, and he dropped on them, his arms holding him up on the bar. Lonnie looked at the shotgun. He looked at Comstock's revolver. Snapper's eyes went blank. His arms slid off the bar and he fell dead on the floor behind it. Comstock looked at Lonnie.

"Put it away," he said.

Lonnie reached slowly for the shotgun. He put three fingers on the barrel and eased it around until it was pointed safely away from the sheriff. Then he let down the hammer and put the shotgun away under the bar.

"We'll have to check into the ownership of this place tomorrow," Comstock said. He put away his six-gun and walked to the door. Then he turned back toward his deputies. "First thing in the morning, boys," he said.

# 21

When Slocum woke up the following morning, he was craving a good cup of coffee, maybe even a good breakfast of eggs and ham and potatoes and gravy, biscuits, all the good things that one could have in the morning. He decided that it couldn't hurt anything to pay a discreet visit to the Snug T, just long enough to get a good meal and to check up on everyone, make sure they were all doing okay. He pulled on his boots, strapped on his Colt and put his hat on his head. Then he saddled the Appaloosa. He rolled up his blankets and tied them on behind the saddle. He had not built a fire, so he had little to do in obliterating evidence that he had stopped there for the night. He mounted up and headed for the ranch.

He kept his eyes open riding toward the ranch, in the event that Comstock and crew were out on the prowl, but he did not really expect to see them. He had not seen any of them for some time except for the time when he had beat up the sheriff, and he wondered what they had been up to. He would find out at the Snug T. He would be there before too much longer. He was thinking that it was about time for him to finish this mess. The longer he waited, the more chance Comstock would have of hiring on more men, and Slocum already had five of them to deal with. The more men Comstock had, the more chances that someone else would be drawn in on the fight. Slocum did not want that.

Comstock had actually managed to get his four deputies up and around early. They'd had their breakfast and were mounted up in front of the sheriff's office at the crack of dawn. In fact, they'd had to wait a little for the sheriff to finish getting himself ready to ride with them, but at last they were on their way out to the Snug T.

"You boys just leave all the talking up to me," Comstock said as they rode along.

"Sure thing, Boss," said Slab. "What if we see that Slocum out there?"

"In that case, just do what I already told you to do. Kill the son of a bitch. We'll be looking for him anyhow. That's the reason for going out there. That and just to get a look around and kind of see what their strength is. Keep that in mind, too."

"You boys all got that?" said Slab.

"We got ears," said Art Bacon.

They made the rest of the trip in silence. When they reached the Snug T, they made straight for the main ranch house. Chaney and Pearlie must have heard them coming, for as the lawmen rode up to the porch, the two of them stepped out of the house. Chaney's six-gun was strapped on, and Pearlie held a rifle at her side.

"Comstock," said Chaney, "what are you doing here?"

"I come on business," said the sheriff.

"You got no business here," said Pearlie. "You already collected your dirty tax money."

"I didn't come out here on account of taxes, missy," said Comstock. "I'm looking for a fugitive. I got reason to suspect that you all could be hiding him out here."

"Who's that?" said Chaney.

"Name of Slocum. He used to work for you, I believe. Maybe he still does. What would you say to that?"

"I'd say you're mistaken," Pearlie said. "He no longer

works here, and we haven't seen him. Have you seen him anywhere?"

Comstock reached up and rubbed his swollen eye. "By the looks of you," said Chaney, "I'd say you've see him, and recently."

"If you've seen him since we have," Pearlie added, "what the hell are you doing looking for him out here?"

"Never you mind," Comstock said. "We're going to take us a look around."

Pearlie jerked the rifle up to her shoulder. "You just ride on out of here," she said. "You ain't looking around my home."

A group of cowhands had appeared over by the corral. They were watching the business taking place around the house. Charlie Bob and Flank Steak were out in front. Mixed in with the bunch were the small ranchers who had come to the Snug T for safety. When they saw Pearlie raise her rifle, they started walking toward the house. Comstock and his deputies saw them, too. Slab's right hand was perched, ready to slap leather.

"Hold it, boys," said Comstock. "We didn't come out here looking for trouble. Al, Miss Pearlie, I was hoping for a little more cooperation from you. All I want is a look around, but I don't mean to force myself on you. If you refuse to co-operate, we'll just be riding back into town, but I'll have to assume that you are for a fact hiding Slocum around here somewhere. I'll get me a warrant and come back again. Course, he'll most likely be long gone by then."

"We told you he ain't here," said Chaney.

"Wait a minute, Comstock," said Pearlie. She lowered her rifle. "All right. Get down and take your look around. Satisfy yourself. I don't want to see you out here again."

Comstock glanced over at the large group of cowhands. He and his boys were outnumbered, that was for sure. He did not think that the Snug T had such a large crew. Then he recognized a couple of the small ranchers. So they had not fled the county. They had fled to the Snug T. He was glad that Pearlie had relented. He did not want to risk a fight, not just then and not at that place. Swinging down out of the saddle, he said, "Come on, boys. You heard the lady." The deputies all got down and followed Comstock up onto the porch. The sheriff looked at the front door and then at Pearlie.

"Go on," she said. He opened the door and went inside, followed by his four gunmen. They stood there looking around the big living room. Pearlie and Chaney walked in behind them. "You can see he's not in here," said Pearlie. "You'd best look in the other rooms." They walked slowly all through the house. At last they gathered again in the living room.

"He ain't anywhere in here, Boss," said Slab. "We looked in all the closets and everything."

"Let's check the bunkhouse," Comstock said. The Comstock gang and Chaney and Pearlie all walked back out on the porch. The cowhands had come up to the house by this time and were standing on the ground around the porch. Comstock and his bunch stood ready for anything that might happen. They were obviously nervous.

"Charlie Bob," said Chaney, "the sheriff and his men want to look around. Let them look."

Charlie Bob shrugged, and Comstock led the way to the bunkhouse. In a few minutes, he and his deputies came back out. They walked back to the house, where their horses waited.

"Satisfied?" said Pearlie.

"You got line shacks," Comstock said.

"You know where they are. Ride on out to them and look if you want to," Pearlie said.

The sheriff's gang mounted up. "We'll do that," said Comstock. He turned his horse and, followed by his gang, headed for the main gate and the road. The Snug T outfit watched them ride off.

"If it had been up to me," Flank Steak said, "we'd have killed them all."

"Why didn't we?" Chaney asked. "The governor made them outlaws, didn't he?"

"Some of our boys might've got hurt," said Pearlie. "We'll make a plan and take them our own way in our own time."

Comstock did not say a word until they had reached the road. Then he said, "God damn it, boys, did you see what I seen?"

"Slocum?" said Hack McGuire.

"No," said Comstock. "He wasn't nowhere around. In that bunch of cowhands was them small ranchers that we thought we'd run off. They come over here. They're planning something. We'd better get back to town and wait for that marshal and his deputies. There's too damn many of them for us to fight it out with."

"I thought that was a pretty damn big ranch crew," said Slab.

"Well, it ain't no ranch crew," Comstock said. "It's all the damn ranchers in this valley, and then some. Come on. Let's make tracks."

Without waiting for a response, he kicked his horse in the sides and hurried on down the road. The others followed his lead. They were riding hard when they rounded a bend in the road and ran smack into Slocum headed for the Snug T. He was as surprised as they were. So was his horse. The big Appaloosa reared, throwing Slocum slightly off balance. He fought for control of his horse, reached for his Winchester and headed for the side of the road. The Comstock gang reacted in basically the same way. When they got off the road, they dismounted, grabbed whatever cover they could find and started shooting.

Slocum had gotten himself behind a large tree in a clump of trees, and he was looking for a target. Everyone was snugged down pretty good though. A bullet hit the tree trunk and zinged by his head. He pressed his back against the trunk. There were five of them out there, all shooting. He couldn't get a peek around the tree to look for them. His horse had moved toward the back of the trees on its own. Slocum decided that the best thing to do was run for his life. Even if he could find one target and get a shot at it, the others would likely pick him off. He cursed himself for his carelessness. Then he got down on his hands and knees and crawled toward his horse.

He stayed down as low as he could. The bullets were still sounding behind him, but he did not think that anyone had actually spotted him crawling along. He made it to his horse and got up slowly, looking back toward the road. Quickly then, he mounted up and rode hard out across the prairie. The dumb deputies were still firing at the clump of trees. He rode the long way around to find a high spot from which he could survey the scene he had just left. From his new vantage point, he could see the deputies emerge from their hiding places. He saw Comstock mount his horse and wave his arms around giving orders. Slocum pulled out his Winchester and raised it. Then he lowered it again. The range was too great. He would only waste a shot.

Down below, Comstock had the deputies searching the small patch of woods.

"We got him," he said. "The shooting stopped."

"Look over that way," Slab said to McGuire. "Look all around."

"Find him," Comstock shouted. "I want to see his body."

In another couple of minutes, Slab came back out onto the road, followed by the other three. Comstock said, "Well?"

"He ain't in there, Boss," said Slab. "His horse is gone. Somehow he got away from us."

"Damn," said Comstock.

"You want us to go after him?"

"It's too dangerous out here so close to the Snug T," the sheriff said. "No. I got to think. Let's get our ass into town."

Up on the nearby rise, Slocum thought again about wasting a shot. He decided it would not be wasted after all. It would put some fear into the wretched gang. He cranked a shell into the chamber and raised the rifle to his shoulder. He took careful aim at the biggest and easiest target. He did not think that he would hit it, but it would kick up dust in among them and give them a fright. He squeezed the trigger.

Spike Allen yelped loud as a slug tore through his upper right thigh.

"Let's go," screamed Comstock, and the gang rode hard toward Hangout.

Slocum smiled as he put away his rifle. He waited a moment. Then, satisfied that the sheriff and his crew were headed back to town, he turned his horse toward the Snug T.

Pearlie and Chaney were on the porch talking to the entire assembly there at the ranch, the whole group of Snug T riders and refugee small ranchers. Some of the group had wanted to know why they had not taken the crooked sheriff and his men while they had a chance. Pearlie was trying to explain.

"We're not gunfighters out here," she said. "We're ranchers and cowboys. There's no sense in any one of us getting shot. Not when there's a U.S. marshal and his deputies on their way to Hangout. I say we let the law handle them."

"It's the law that's been robbing us blind," someone shouted.

"And killing some," said another.

Pearlie held up her hands for silence. "Don't you think I know that?" she said. "My own uncle was killed by those murderers. I haven't forgotten that, not for a minute. Comstock is a crooked sheriff. He's not the law. He's an outlaw, him and the rest of his gang, and even though he doesn't know it yet, the governor does. The governor has declared them outlaws and is sending some real lawmen down here to take care of this whole mess. They should be here tomorrow, maybe even later on today. Hold on for just a little longer."

She looked over the crowd standing below her and saw a rider coming. She waited just a little and recognized Slocum. When he drew closer, she waved and shouted.

"Slocum, Come on in."

Molly stepped out of the crowd to the rear to wait. Slocum rode on up and dismounted. Molly stepped up to greet him, and he put an arm around her shoulders and started walking through the crowd toward the porch. When he reached the steps, he turned loose of Molly and moved up onto the porch.

"Slocum," said Pearlie. "Damn, I'm glad you're back."

"Me, too," said Chaney.

"What happened out here?" Slocum asked. "I just ran into Comstock and his crowd on the road. Looked like they was coming from here."

"They came here looking for you," Pearlie said. "I let them look around. They didn't start any trouble. Just rode off."

"I reckon they looked at our numbers here and decided against starting anything," said Chaney.

"Yeah," said Slocum. "That's likely."

"But, Slocum," said Pearlie, "we've got some good news."

"Big news," said Chaney.

Pearlie then filled Slocum in on her trip to the capital. She told him how Comstock had stopped them and turned them back on the road and how they had then gone around the long way, and she told him how the governor had accepted her story about the way things had been happening in the valley around Hangout. The governor, she said, had declared Comstock and his gang outlaws, and he was sending a federal posse to take care of them.

"You're not a fugitive anymore," she said. "You're not wanted."

"It's all over," Chaney said. "All we have to do is sit tight out here and wait for the marshal and his posse to ride in and clean up."

Slocum sat down heavily in the nearest chair and shoved back his hat.

"Well," he said, "is there any chance of getting a meal and some good hot coffee around here?"

# 22

Slocum ate his fill and enjoyed every bite. He drank six cups of coffee, and finally he went out on the porch and smoked a cigar. Chaney went on to direct the cowhands, and in a couple of minutes, Pearlie came out on the porch to visit with Slocum. She asked him if he intended to stick around and work on the ranch. After all, there was nothing left for him to do in regards to Comstock and that bunch. The U.S. marshal would take care of all that. He told her that he would probably just wander on. After he had gotten himself involved in violence, he did not like to hang around a place. It seemed as if he could not live a normal life in a town where he had done killing, even if it was justified. But he was thinking the whole time. He had no intention of leaving Comstock to the marshal. He had been there when Comstock murdered poor old Tyson. He had witnessed the brutality of it all. He had sworn that he would get the man, and he intended to keep his word. He saw no reason, however, to say anything to Pearlie about it. When he had finished his smoke, he stood up. The Appaloosa was still saddled. Everything he owned was either on its back or on his own.

"Well, Pearlie," he said, "I guess I'll be moving on."

"So soon?" she said. "Just like that?"

"Like you said, my work's all done here. Let the law take care of the rest."

"You know you've got a job here as long as you want it."

"Thanks, but I'll just be on my way."

"If you ever change your mind, the job will still be open."

He went down the stairs and mounted his horse. Giving her one last look, he tipped his hat, turned and rode away. He did not look back. When he rode out the big main gate, he turned toward Hangout. He did not have a definite plan. He only meant that Comstock should not be alive when he left the valley. He moved along easily, riding at his leisure, as if he were going to a church picnic. He knew already that his Colt and his Winchester were both ready for action, and he figured that they would both find plenty of it up ahead. He did not care so much about the so-called deputies. They were all new. They had not been around when Tyson was killed. The law could take care of them for all he cared. He just wanted Comstock. But he thought that he might have to kill them, at least some of them, in order to get to Comstock. Well, he would deal with it when the time came. Let them deal the cards.

When Slocum reached Hangout, he still rode straight and easy, but his eyes shifted from one side of the street to the other, even up to the rooftops. He had no idea where he would locate Comstock. He might be in his office or in the Bird's Beak Saloon. It was a little early yet for the saloon, but with that bunch you could never tell. He decided that he would try the sheriff's office first. Suddenly he saw his way blocked by a man standing in the middle of the street and looking straight at him. He recognized the man as one of the new deputies, but he did not know the man's name. He stopped riding and sat giving the man back his stare.

It was Art Bacon. Bacon fancied himself quite a gunslinger. No Slocum or anyone else was going to intimidate him. He was thinking about the one thousand dollars Comstock had promised, and he had no intention of sharing it with anyone. It was his good fortune to have been out in the street alone when Slocum came riding in.

Without taking his eyes off the man, Slocum dismounted

and slapped the Appaloosa's rump. The big stallion trotted off to a side of the street. Slocum stood facing Bacon.

"I don't know you, mister," he said. "We don't have to fight."

"You're worth a thousand dollars to me," said Bacon.

"You can't spend it from the grave."

"A man ought to know who's killing him. I'm Art Bacon."

"Never heard of you, and I'll forget your name by the time you hit the ground."

Bacon slapped leather without another word. He was fast. He had cleared his holster before Slocum went for his gun, but his first shot went wild to the left. He thumbed back the hammer for a second shot, but Slocum fired first that time. Slocum's slug smashed Bacon's right shoulder. Bacon yelled and dropped his six-gun. Slocum holstered his Colt. Bacon dropped to his knees, blood running freely from the fresh shoulder wound, and reached for his revolver with his left hand. Quickly, Slocum drew his Colt and fired again. This time the bullet went straight into Bacon's heart, and the gunman pitched forward on his face, dead.

The gunfire attracted the attention of Comstock and his other three deputies inside the sheriff's office. Slab opened the door to look out and saw Slocum standing over the corpse of Bacon. Slocum looked around and caught a glimpse of Slab, but just as he did, Slab shut the door again.

Inside the office, Slab said, "It's Slocum. He just killed Art."

"Get him," said Comstock.

Slab, Spike Allen and Hack McGuire all grabbed rifles from the rack on the wall. They smashed out the front windows of the sheriff's office. Out in the street, Slocum saw what was happening and ran for the cover of a nearby watering trough, ducking down behind it just as a bullet smashed into it. Then the bullets started flying. Slocum stayed hunkered down as they spanged into the trough.

"Don't waste your shots," Comstock said. The firing slowed down and then stopped. Slocum seized the opportunity and ran for the nearest building corner, ducking around its edge just as another bullet struck the wall behind him.

"Where'd he go?" said Slab.

"He's just around that corner there," said McGuire. "The general store."

From his cover, Slocum raised up his Colt and fired into the window of the sheriff's office, striking a piece of the already broken window glass and sending shards over Slab's face. Slab yelped and stepped back. His face was cut in several places.

"Son of a bitch," he said.

Slocum ducked quickly back around the corner as bullets struck the wall near him. He dumped the empty cartridges from the chamber of his Colt and replaced them with fresh bullets.

"Any ideas?" said Slab.

It was silent there in the sheriff's office for a moment. Comstock looked around, peeping out the window carefully. Then he stepped back to the center of the room.

"There's a way up onto the roof behind the building next door," he said. "Someone could get a good shot at him from up there."

"I'll go," said Hack McGuire, and he ran out the back door before anyone could agree or disagree.

Out at the Snug T, Chaney had gone back to the house. When he saw Pearlie, he asked where Slocum had gone. She told him what Slocum had said to her, that he was leaving the county, leaving the cleanup work to the law. Chaney shrugged. He gave Pearlie a quick kiss and said, "Charlie Bob and Flank Steak's waiting for me outside. I better get going." When he walked out onto the porch, Pearlie followed him out.

"Where's Slocum?" said Flank Steak.

"He's left the county," said Chaney.

"With Comstock still alive?" said Flank Steak. "I don't believe that for a minute."

"You think—"

"I'd say he's gone to town to kill that snake."

"Get my horse," said Pearlie. "We've got to get in there and give him a hand."

Hack McGuire crawled on his belly along the roof of the store until he reached the front edge. The building had a facade that rose three feet above the roof. McGuire reached the facade and raised his head slowly until he could peek over its edge. It took him a moment to locate Slocum, and then he did not have a clear shot. He could barely make out where Slocum was located from the edge of his elbow showing around the corner. He would have to do something to get a good shot. Just then someone in the sheriff's office fired a couple. When they stopped shooting, Slocum showed himself just long enough to snap off another shot at the window. When he did that, McGuire raised himself, his rifle at his shoulder, and fired.

The shot tore Slocum's hat off his head as he ducked back around the corner. "Damn," he said. The shot had been way too close for comfort. He knew then that there was someone on the roof across the street, next door to the sheriff's office. He had a good idea about where the man was located, but the high facade hid him; he could have moved. Slocum wished that he had carried his Winchester with him. Well, he had drawn the man's fire once. He could do it again the same way; only this time, he would be expecting the man. He stepped out to fire a shot at the window, and when he did, McGuire raised himself again. Slocum swung his gun hand around and fired a round at McGuire. The bullet smashed into McGuire's forehead just above and between the eyes, and he slumped forward, laying over the facade. Slocum was back around the corner again as bullets from the windows of the sheriff's office smacked against the wall.

Slocum took time to reload again. Then he ran around behind the building and came out on the other side, sneaking along through the narrow path between the two buildings until he was again at a corner on the street.

Inside the sheriff's office, Comstock, Slab and Spike Allen were still focusing on the corner Slocum had already vacated. They had no idea he had shifted positions.

"He ain't fired for a while," said Slab. "You reckon one of us got him?"

"I wouldn't count on it," said Comstock.

"If one of us got him," said Allen, "but we don't know who it was, do we split the thousand?"

"Yes. Yes. Hell, I don't give a damn," said Comstock. "Just make sure the son of a bitch is dead."

They were silent for a bit, listening. No shots sounded from the roof above. None from across the street.

"I say he's dead," said Allen.

"You want to go out and check?" said Slab.

"Well, we can't just stand here doing nothing forever."

"So go and check."

"All right," said Allen. "I will, but I ain't going out that front door."

He walked to the back door and stepped out. Looking both directions, he decided that he would go to his right. He walked down two buildings, then turned to move between them. He made his way to the street. Peeking around the corner of the building there, he looked toward the corner across the street where he had last seen Slocum. He could see no one. There was no one at all on the street. Everyone in town had run to a hidey-hole. Allen thought that Slocum could be lying dead there around that corner, and he would not be able to see the body. He decided to investigate. Ducking low, he ran zigzagging across the street and pressed himself flat against the wall of the building there. He waited a moment, then sidled down to the corner where Slocum had been hiding. Quickly, he stepped into the slot between buildings. There was no one there.

Allen stepped out onto the sidewalk holding his arms out to his sides and looking across the street at the sheriff's office. "He ain't here," he called out. Slocum stepped out from his hiding place between the next two buildings.

"I'm here," he said. Allen whirled and raised his shooter, but Slocum fired first, the slug knocking Allen off his feet and onto his back there on the sidewalk. He groaned and lifted his head, getting a look at the blood gushing from his chest. "Damn you," he said, trying to raise himself up. Then his eyes glazed over and he fell back dead. Slocum ducked back and replaced the spent shell.

Inside the office, Slab looked at Comstock. "It's just you and me now," he said. "You got any bright ideas?"

"I hired you on to take care of Slocum for me," Comstock said. "you're the one ought to have a bright idea."

"I'm going out there and give myself up. That's what."

"Why, you chicken shit," said Comstock.

"You ain't going to try to stop me, are you?"

Comstock thought quickly. This might work out to his advantage. "No," he said. "Do what you want."

Slab jerked open the front door, keeping himself clear of the opening. He yelled out from inside the office, "Slocum. You hear me?"

"I hear you," Slocum answered.

"I'm coming out. I don't want to fight you. You and me got no quarrel."

"Throw out your gun," Slocum said.

Slab tossed out his six-shooter. "Okay?"

"Come on out," said Slocum. "I won't shoot you."

Slab stepped out onto the sidewalk with his hands held high. Slocum stayed behind the corner of the building. "Where's Comstock?" he said.

Slab jerked his head back. "He's still in there," he said.

But Comstock had gone out the back door. He hurried as fast as he could go to the stable down the street, went inside through the back, got his horse saddled and mounted up. He did not want to ride past Slocum. He thought that he would ride down the back street to the edge of town and then out, but if he was to ride toward the capital, he would still be too close to Slocum for comfort. He would ride toward the Snug T. He was making his way when he saw Pearlie and the three cowhands riding toward him.

"Shit," he snarled. He hauled back at the reins and turned his mount as fast as he could. There was nothing for it but to go right back through town, right past Slocum, hoping for the best.

The commotion down the road caught Slocum's attention, and he turned to look. When he did, Slab sprang for his own dropped six-gun. Grabbing it up, he turned to fire at Slocum. In the meantime, Comstock was bearing down on Slocum. Slocum took a shot at Comstock, and his bullet tore the sheriff's right ear off. Blood flew. Comstock cursed and pulled out his own six-gun. Slab fired, his bullet just missing and kicking up dust behind Slocum. Slocum turned and shot Slab through the middle of the chest, dropping him dead. By this time, Comstock had a good bead on Slocum. He was about to pull the trigger when Pearlie, her rifle at her shoulder, fired. The slug smashed Comstock's spine, dropping him from his horse's back. His body hit the dirt, raising a cloud of dust around it, flopped once or twice and then lay still.

Pearlie rode on up to Slocum and stopped her horse.

"I thought you were leaving the county," she said.

"I will now," he said. "Was that your shot?"

"Yeah."

"Well, you dropped him good."

"The deputies?" said Pearlie.

"All dead," Slocum said.

"Then it's really for sure damn over," said Flank Steak, who had just ridden up with Chaney and Charlie Bob.

"It's over," said Slocum.

Just then they all turned toward the sound of a half a dozen or more horses riding into town. Slocum and the rest braced themselves for more trouble as they watched seven riders come in. The riders kept moving. They made no moves for their guns though. At last they came close and stopped. The man in the lead looked at the body of Comstock. He looked around and saw Slab on one side of the street and Spike Allen on the other. Then he saw the other two bodies.

"What's happened here?" said the man.

"A showdown," Slocum said. "Who are you?"

"Marshal Brandon, down from the capital. Who might you folks be?"

"I'm Pearlie Tyson. These men all work for me. This one here in the street is the former Sheriff Comstock, and those other carcasses were all his deputies."

Brandon swung down out of the saddle and walked over to Pearlie, extending his hand. "Miss Tyson," he said, "you're the person the governor told me to contact. I'm pleased to meet you. You say you got them all?"

Pearlie looked at Slocum. He nodded.

"We got them all, Marshal," she said.

"Well then," said Brandon, "our job here is all paperwork." He turned to his posse. "Boys," he said, "let's all go over to the saloon. I'm buying." Looking back at Pearlie, he added, "You all are invited, too."

Watch for

**SLOCUM AND THE TETON TEMPTRESS**

310th novel in the exciting SLOCUM
series from Jove

*Coming in December!*

**Explore the exciting Old West with one of the men who made it wild!**

# J. R. ROBERTS

# THE GUNSMITH